Divided City

www.kidsatrandomhouse.co.uk

Also available by Theresa Breslin:

REMEMBRANCE
SASKIA'S JOURNEY

For junior readers:

THE DREAM MASTER
DREAM MASTER NIGHTMARE!
DREAM MASTER GLADIATOR
DREAM MASTER ARABIAN NIGHTS

www.theresabreslin.co.uk

Divided City

THERESA BRESLIN

DOUBLEDAY

London · New York · Toronto · Sydney · Auckland

DIVIDED CITY
A DOUBLEDAY BOOK 0 385 60767 9

Published in Great Britain by Doubleday,
an imprint of Random House Children's Books

This edition published 2005

1 3 5 7 9 10 8 6 4 2

Papers used by Random House Children's Books are natural, recyclable products made from wood grown in sustainable forests. The manufacturing processes conform to the environmental regulations of the country of origin.

Set in 12/15.5pt Bembo Schoolbook by
Falcon Oast Graphic Art Ltd.

RANDOM HOUSE CHILDREN'S BOOKS
61–63 Uxbridge Road, London W5 5SA
A division of The Random House Group Ltd

RANDOM HOUSE AUSTRALIA (PTY) LTD
20 Alfred Street, Milsons Point, Sydney,
New South Wales 2061, Australia

RANDOM HOUSE NEW ZEALAND LTD
18 Poland Road, Glenfield, Auckland 10, New Zealand

RANDOM HOUSE (PTY) LTD
Endulini, 5A Jubilee Road, Parktown 2193, South Africa

THE RANDOM HOUSE GROUP Limited Reg. No. 954009
www.**kidsatrandomhouse**.co.uk

A CIP catalogue record for this book is available from the British Library.

Printed and bound in Great Britain
by Mackays of Chatham plc, Chatham Kent

This book is for Glasgow

Chapter 1

Footsteps.

Running.

Graham didn't hear them at first.

He was walking fast, eating from his bag of hot chips as he went. Taking a detour via Reglan Street. The kind of street his parents had warned him never to be in. The kind of street where your footsteps echoed loud, too loud – because there was no one else about.

From either side the dark openings of the tenement building mawed at him. It was the beginning of May and fairly light at this time in the evening. But even so . . . Graham glanced around. The sky was densely overcast and shadows were gathering. He shouldn't have lingered so long after football training.

Graham dug deep into the bag to find the last chips, the little crispy ones soaked in vinegar that always nestled in the folds of paper at the bottom. He wiped his mouth and, scrunching up the chip paper, he threw it into the air. When it came down he sent it rocketing upwards, powered by his own quality header. The paper ball spun high above him. Graham made a half turn.

Wait for it . . . wait for it . . .

Now.

'Yes!' Graham shouted out loud as his chip bag bounced off a lamppost ten metres away. An ace back-heeler! With a shot like that he could zap a ball past any keeper right into the back of the net. He grinned and thrust his hands in the air to acknowledge the shouts of the fans.

At that moment noise and shouting erupted behind him, and Graham knew right away that he was in trouble.

Footsteps.

Running.

Coming down Reglan Street. Hard. Desperate.

Pounding on the ground. Beyond them, further away, whooping yells and shouts.

'Get the scum! Asylum scum!'

Graham turned. A teenage boy was racing towards him. As Graham watched, the boy stumbled, tripped and fell. Tried to get up. Then, groping in his pocket, brought out a mobile phone. Started to dial, changed his mind. Looking round in panic.

At the end of Reglan Street nearest the playing fields, huge shadows danced. The outline of the hunters – distorted and elongated against the bright floodlights used for night games on the football pitches. Graham saw them gather together, become one monstrous creature, then break apart. Their twisted shapes thrown out ahead of them as they came. Seeking. Searching.

Graham's legs stopped working. He was too far from

the main road. Too far to run. This gang would catch him easily.

The boy got to his feet. Faltered. Went past Graham. Limping.

Now Graham was caught. Trapped between pursuer and pursued.

If he began to run the gang of boys would think he was running from them – might mistake him for the one they were after. His heart was hammering. He didn't want to get involved in this.

He had to get off the street, find somewhere to hide. If he could get into one of the tenements and through to the other side, there might be a way out across the backs. Over a wall and down the maze of lanes and alleys between the buildings.

The victim had the same idea. Graham saw the boy stagger into one of the close entrances.

One of the gang ran past Graham, shoving him roughly aside. His face shone with sweat and excitement.

The baying of the other boys sounded nearer, shouting and jeering.

'Scum! Scum!'

And then a string of swear words.

Graham jumped onto the pavement and over to the entrance nearest him. Most tenements and blocks of flats didn't have open entries any more. But often, especially in areas like this, they'd be lying ajar because people didn't bother, or the door catch was broken. This one was locked firm against him.

Graham pressed himself against the door, glad of his skinny frame. The remainder of the gang came down the street, veering onto the pavement as they spotted him.

One of them pushed his face up against Graham's. 'Where'd he go? Where'd he go?'

He had a knife in his hand.

Graham's eyes widened in terror. He couldn't speak, couldn't take his gaze from the knife. The boy raised his knife. 'Speak, ya wee—'

Graham shook his head. The older boy was half out of it with drink or drugs or both. The rest of them ran on. They shouted from further down the street.

'We've got him! He's here!'

Graham crouched in the doorway. He heard them dragging the boy from his hiding place. The thudding sound of someone being kicked. If he covered his ears perhaps he wouldn't hear. Graham wrapped his hands and arms all the way round his head. To block out the sound. The noise. Grunting laughter of the attackers.

He waited. Whimpering.

Nothing. No scream. No cry for help.

Then footsteps. Running away. Diminishing.

Graham took his hands from his head. He stepped from the doorway onto the street. Went slowly forward to look at the huddled body lying on the ground. Beside the paper ball of his chip bag there was a puddle of liquid. Under the light of the street lamp it reflected dull red. It was seeping from below the body of the boy. Moving out towards Graham's feet.

A dark stain spreading.

Chapter 2

Joseph Flaherty – Joe to his friends – also made a chip-shop stop that evening.

Like Graham, he didn't go straight home after football training on a Friday either. Instead, Joe went into the city centre to earn some pocket money at his aunt's hair-dressing shop. Not that he'd be seen dead in the place when it was open. Too many women clack-clacking away. But on Friday night he dropped by to help tidy up after their late opening and get things ready for the busy Saturday. The shop was on the corner of the Gallowgate and High Street. It was his granny's shop really, but his gran was getting too old to do much, so it was mainly Joe's Aunt Kathleen, his dad's youngest sister, who ran the place. And on a Friday night the two women were always keen to finish and catch the last bingo session at the Forge. So it was Joe who did most of the clearing up by himself. He preferred it that way. He'd pull the outside steel shutter down, lock himself in the shop and put his music on.

He got off the bus at the Tron and went into a nearby chip shop.

'Got them ready for you, Joey.' The shop owner smiled at the boy as he pushed open the door.

Joe took the bag of chips, pulled out the top one, blew on it and bit off the end. The hot vinegary taste seared his tongue and he took a quick drink from a can of Irn-Bru to cool his mouth. He chatted to Sergio for a while about the football. The Italian was a Celtic supporter, though there was nothing in the shop to let you know that. No colours or badges or magazines like the *Celtic View* lying on the counter. Wouldn't take the risk of antagonizing any customers who might support the other side. Joe asked him if he was going to the Celtic v Rangers match tomorrow.

'No one to cover for the shop,' said Sergio. 'And I wouldn't close up. I do good business on the day of an Old Firm game.'

They talked of Celtic's chances. Joe was confident, but Sergio shook his head.

'Carmichael's a great new player,' he said, 'but that latest signing from Italy has me worried.'

'I thought Italians could play better than anyone in the world?' said Joe.

'So they can,' said Sergio. 'But he is Calabrese.'

Joe laughed. 'What's wrong with the Calabrese?'

Sergio narrowed his eyes and clicked his tongue against the back of his teeth. 'They are Calabrese,' he said.

Joe told him about the goal his team had scored in the last minutes of tonight's game.

'We thought we'd get slaughtered. We've never played against a proper eleven-a-side opposition before. But our defence stood up to them, and we stole the game in the last seconds. I think Jack Burns, the coach, had his eye on me. Well, me and this other boy, Graham. I'm hoping I get picked for the Glasgow City first team. We've a whole set of trials to get through. The sessions are next Wednesday and Friday, and the first game of the tournament is a week on Sunday. Glasgow's been drawn against Liverpool in the first leg. Just think, Sergio. I might be in the team that represents Glasgow! All the cities in the UK are taking part. It's a new Cup, a Gold Cup, the UK Inter-Cities Youth Team Gold Cup.'

'Sounds exciting,' said Sergio, not letting on that Joe had told him about the Gold Cup every single week for the past few months.

'And tonight's goal. It was ace,' Joe went on, his eyes glowing. 'This is me' – he picked up a bottle of tomato sauce – 'and this' – he pointed to the vinegar bottle – 'is my team-mate, Graham.'

Sergio watched as Joe, using the jars of pickled onions as goalposts, described the goal. 'Looks like what Harald Brattbakk did against St Johnstone when Celtic won the League in nineteen ninety-eight,' he commented. 'I was at that match. Brattbakk came haring down the field to pick up a cross from Jackie McNamara and blasted it into the back of the net.'

'*Exactly* like that,' said Joe. 'I got the pass across to Graham at the right time. And you should have seen him thump it away. He's a brilliant player.'

'But you put the ball at his feet,' said Sergio loyally. He tapped his head. 'That type of play takes brains as well as skill.'

'To tell you the truth, I can't say I thought it out,' said Joe. 'It was more like instinct. I just knew he'd move into position. And he told me afterwards that he sensed that I would bring the ball to him. We understand each other.'

Joe finished his chips as he walked towards his granny's shop. Draining the last of his Irn-Bru, he lobbed the can into the air ahead of him. He caught it with his foot as it returned to earth, and then began to dribble the empty can along the street.

A high kick from Scotland's captain. It's a loose ball. Anybody's. But here's Flaherty! Joseph Flaherty, Scotland's hero, has captured the ball!

Nothing could stop him now.

The glitter of gold was upon him.

The commentator's voice rose to a shriek.

Joe Flaherty is storming down the field! This undersize, underage, football player from Glasgow has full mastery of the ball. Demonstrating incredible talent from someone of his age! Although he is years younger than his team-mates, the international squad insisted he should be included. Only months ago, at an extraordinary meeting of the Scottish Football Association the board unanimously agreed that this boy from the great city of Glasgow should be allowed to play for Scotland. And now, in this final of the World Cup, they've been proved right.

The streets of the Garngath, Joe's part of the city, are empty tonight. Every single resident is in front of a TV or listening to a radio. Special screens have been set up all over the city. In George Square the match is being beamed onto the front wall of the Glasgow City Chambers. The great and the good have gathered, mingling with ordinary folk. Sharing a bench with a grandstand view of the park are the Lord Provost of the city, J. K. Rowling and Ewan McGregor, watching this nail-biting final together with Joe's dad, granny and Auntie Kathleen.

Despite a brutal tackle, Flaherty is still up and running! Cutting his way through the defence. It's a miracle how he manages it! In previous rounds he astounded Argentina, jinked round the Germans and bamboozled Brazil. Now he's doing it again! No one can touch him!

He's heading straight for the goal mouth! The keeper runs out to meet the attack as he sees the approach of this human fireball. Flaherty feints to the left. The ball rockets from the toe of Flaherty's boot. The keeper leaps to save it. But the ball is curving towards the RIGHT-hand corner. The keeper has dived the wrong way! The ball goes whizzing past his ear. Blootered into the back of the net! What skill! What amazing dexterity! What cunning! Flaherty sent the keeper for a fish supper and drove the winner home!

It's a goal! It's a goal!

There goes the final whistle!

Yes! Yes! Yes!

Scotland has won the World Cup! And it's all down to a goal from Joe Flaherty.

The park is in an uproar!

Garngath has gone mental. Up on the hill where Joe lives they are pouring out onto the streets, singing and dancing. People are weeping in George Square. Joe's granny is hugging the Lord Provost. His Auntie Kathleen has kissed Ewan McGregor.

Back to the pitch.

'Flaherty! Flaherty!'

They want Joe Flaherty. They are cheering themselves hoarse. Joe steps out onto the pitch. They chant their hero's name. Now, to the tune of 'Skip to My Lou', they are singing specially for him . . .

'Joe! Joe! Super Joe!
Joe! Joe! Super Joe!
Joe! Joe! Super Joe!
Su-per Jo-seph Fla-her-ty!'

Modestly Joe raises his arms to wave to the crowd.

'See you!' A voice screeched from above Joe's head. 'I'll stoat your heid off that wall if you kick a can at ma windae again!'

Chapter 3

Graham's breath was coming in great ragged gasps.

The boy on the ground was bleeding. He'd been stabbed!

Graham saw blood pooling slowly beside his body. Real blood. Graham knelt down.

Basic first aid wasn't going to cover this. It needed a doctor . . . an ambulance. The boy's mobile phone was lying in the gutter. Graham picked it up. He tried to steady his breathing. His fingers stabbed at the numbers. 999. He asked for an ambulance and gabbled out the location. When the operator began to talk to him he cut off the power.

Still kneeling, Graham looked up and down the street. It was empty. He could just leave and no one would know he'd been here. There was nothing more he could do. He began to get up.

As he did so the boy's eyes opened and he recoiled in fear.

'It's OK,' said Graham. 'I'm not going to hurt you.'

'You're not one of them?'

'No,' Graham replied hoarsely. The boy's jacket was

open. The front of his T-shirt was sodden with blood. 'You'll be all right,' he went on. 'I've phoned an ambulance.'

The boy gripped Graham's arm. 'No police. Please. No police.'

'Not the police, the ambulance,' said Graham. 'I think you're hurt quite bad.'

'I too believe I am hurt badly.'

'Why did they attack you? Are you in a gang?'

'I am not in a gang.'

'What did you do to annoy them?' asked Graham.

'I breathe.'

What did the boy mean, 'I breathe'? Everybody breathed. Graham shook his head to show he didn't understand, but the boy's eyes were drooping closed. 'Bog it. Bog it. Bog it,' Graham said under his breath. Why did this have to happen now when tonight had been almost perfect?

His football training session earlier had been great. Fantastic. The best ever. Their first proper game against a local senior boy's club and he'd scored a goal!

Right at the end he collected a pass from the fair-haired boy who, like Graham, never missed a training session. A neat cross, landing right at Graham's feet. They had trained regularly together since this special football training had started, yet rarely played on the same side. But tonight the coach, Jack Burns, had decided they should play together for this match, Graham in centre mid-field and the other boy in defence. The boy – Graham only knew him as Joe – had come up on the wing in the dying minutes of a no-score match. A frustrating game against a team of boys who were technically better and heavier, but Graham's team had held them off for an hour and more. And then, at the death, it happened. A long kick-out from the keeper, picked up by Joe, and, suddenly, there's electricity in the air. Eyes on the ball, Joe swept downfield, running towards the by-line.

Watching the ball arc against the evening sky, Graham felt time draw out . . . slow down. Saw the opening. Even before Joe pulled down the ball, Graham was racing through the defence. Hardly checking what was happening elsewhere; only thinking, If there's a break, if by some miracle the ball is in that space just as I arrive, I'll be ready to take advantage. He sensed rather than saw what Joe was doing. Only knew he had to be there to capture the pass if it came. And there it was! A squared cross from Joe. The ball travelling to Graham's feet. Set up for him. Clear path to goal.

Running in, directly in front of the goal mouth, Graham walloped it from twenty metres. Their keeper hesitated for a fraction of time. Caught out! Graham put every ounce of energy into the shot. And scored! By the time the keeper turns, Graham's ball is travelling through that nano-second of time. Past his head. Into the back of the net.

Goal! Goal! Goal!

Graham's heart exploded. He leaped two metres into the air. He punched his fist to the sky.

Goal! Goal! Goal!

The ref blew the whistle. It was the first competitive game they'd played. And they'd won!

Goal! Goal! Goal!

Graham fell to his knees on the turf.

Goal! Goal! Goal!

He thought he was actually going to cry.

Then he scrambled to his feet.

Everyone danced around him. Slapping him on the back. Thumping his shoulders.

Afterwards, in the showers, Graham saw that he'd more bruises from his team-mates punching him than from the game itself.

And in the dressing room the fair-haired boy congratulated him with the rest. 'That was a great shot.'

Graham stood back. 'You set it up,' he said.

The boy nodded. 'Playing blind, I was, like. But I just knew you'd be there.'

'Me too,' laughed Graham. 'Pure instinct. That's what took me to it. Ready for you delivering.'

The boy held out his hand. 'Joe,' he said. 'Joseph Flaherty.'

Graham blinked. He must be the boy from St Veronica's. The Catholic school. The Roman Catholic school. The people his Granda Reid didn't like him to have close contact with. He took the other boy's hand. Shook it. 'Graham,' he replied. 'Graham Anderson.' Then all the rest were crowding round him in the dressing room. Just before he left, Graham heard Jack Burns, the coach, say it was a terrific finish.

But now Graham's night looked like finishing in ruins. Nearly mugged himself, witness to a knifing, wobbly and scared, he hunkered down beside the wounded boy feeling useless that he couldn't do more to help him. The bleeding seemed to have eased off, but maybe he should put a hanky or something against the boy's chest? Graham inched closer and then lifted his head. A siren sounded in the distance. The ambulance he had called was on its way!

'I need to go before the paramedics arrive,' he whispered. 'Otherwise my parents will find out I was here. Then I'll be in a lot of trouble.'

The boy's eyes opened. He tightened his hold on Graham. 'We are brothers then,' he said. 'I also am in trouble.'

'OK.' Graham patted the boy's hand. 'You'll be OK.'

'Please.' The boy spoke again. 'Please don't leave me. I do not want to die alone.'

'You're not going to die.'

'I need something.'

'You need an ambulance, and it's on its way.'

'No – something else.'

'What?'

'I need you to return that phone to someone for me. A girl.'

'What?' said Graham again. He glanced at the boy's mobile, still grasped in his hand.

'And let her know where I am.'

'I can't do that,' said Graham. 'I've got to get home.'

'Please, I beg you. Listen. I had arranged to meet a girl. She won't know what has happened to me. All I want you to do is to give her back her phone and tell her I was attacked. Go to her house tomorrow and do this.'

'I can't.'

'I'm dying. It is my last request. You should honour a dying person's wish.'

Graham looked at the boy in fright. Was he really going to die?

'Do you have paper and pencil? I will write her address. Hurry,' the boy urged Graham. 'Please. There's not much time.'

Graham got one of his school notebooks and a pencil from his bag. He had to support the boy's arm as he wrote.

'The girl is Leanne,' the boy said. 'She lives in High Street. A big house with a garden. We love each other but her parents would not want us to be together.'

'But—' Graham began.

'Look, see. I've written here asking her to give you fifty pounds if you deliver her phone and this message.'

'Fifty pounds!' said Graham. 'No way! It's drugs, isn't it? I don't want anything to do with this.'

'I swear it is nothing to do with drugs. I love the girl. She loves me. We meet secretly. I am on my way to see her. These boys follow me. They attack me. I have done nothing wrong. Please tell Leanne why I did not meet her tonight. If you don't she will have no way of knowing where I am.'

'You could get someone in the hospital to phone her,' said Graham.

'I will tell them nothing in the hospital. Not even my name.'

'What *is* your name?'

The boy looked at Graham from half-shut lids. 'Between us only?'

Graham nodded and bent closer.

'Kyoul. My name is Kyoul.'

At that moment an ambulance, blue light flashing, turned off the main road into Reglan Street.

Chapter 4

'It'll be pure murder in here next Friday,' said Joe's Aunt Kathleen.

'Why specially next Friday?' said Joe, as he followed his aunt around the hairdresser's shop helping her collect in hand mirrors and treatment bottles.

'There's an Orange Walk going past here next Saturday.'

'Of course,' said Joe, 'it's May now. They've started already, haven't they?'

'Oh aye,' said Kathleen. 'They like to get all their wee marches done before the big one in July.'

'We got a note through,' said Joe's granny, 'from the polis. This march, some local one, is a week tomorrow.'

'All the shopkeepers on the route have been told. Most of them'll close up for an hour or two,' said Kathleen.

'I told our Saturday regulars,' said Joe's granny, who was counting out his money onto the counter. 'And a lot of them have changed their appointments. We'll be jam packed next Friday evening. So try and get here as quick as you can, son.'

'Aye,' explained Kathleen, 'some of them, especially the old buddies, won't come out on a Saturday if there's a march on.' She placed the things she had gathered behind the desk and went to put on her coat. 'Don't forget the towels, Joe, will you?'

'I won't forget,' Joe said.

He was still thinking about this evening's football as he stuffed the wet towels into the washing machine at the back of the shop. Fabulous game! He'd been well pleased to be picked out for the trials when the coach had visited his school all those months ago. He'd take *any* opportunity to play football . . . or watch it. He didn't really know what made football different from other sports. Last term one of his teachers asked the class to write an essay on their favourite sport. She said it wasn't enough to merely write of their experiences as a player or spectator. You'd to go deeper than that. Find the *why*, she'd told them.

The *why*. Joe had puzzled over it for ages. What *was* the appeal of football over everything else? He knew people called it 'the beautiful game'. But why? Joe ended up having a big long discussion with his dad. His dad had followed Celtic since he was a young boy. Knew the teams, the games, the years they'd won and lost. Could rhyme off the names of the players who had brought the European Cup back to Glasgow from Lisbon. They'd talked for hours about all the various aspects of the game. What made it special? Sometimes there was an exceptional player, like Henrik Larsson. He was special. You watched him, followed him, and he made you feel special too. The game was individual, it was team. It was single, it was crowd. It was physical, but you needed to use your brain. It was skill. It was instinctive. Joe had got an A for that essay.

Instinctive. In the game earlier tonight both he and the other boy's play had been instinctive. Joe went over the moves again as he began to sweep up the floor. Wondering how he had known, without looking up, without thinking, that the taller boy would go racing up the park. When he'd first taken possession of the ball Joe thought to try to make the run and the shot himself, but knew that the team's best chance was for him to pass to someone in a better position. Jack Burns, the coach, gave them a talk on this every training night. This new youth team he was building, Glasgow City, would be great, he said – as a team. They had to play as a unit. It had been good of Graham, the goal scorer, to give him some credit though. Decent of him to acknowledge that Joe had set it up.

But . . . Joe recalled how the other boy had hesitated just for a second before shaking his hand. And he knew why.

They talked about it in his family. The way some people reacted as soon as they heard your name, or the name of the school that you went to. You might as well be wearing a label. CATHOLIC. Branded on your forehead. You saw them clock it. And then the look as they slotted you into a box inside their head. And what they thought of you depended on the dimensions of that box.

'It really gets to me the way some people feel free to make remarks about the size of your family and actually believe that you might sympathize with child-murdering terrorists,' Joe had heard his Aunt Kathleen ranting on to his father one day. 'In the shop even, by my own customers, I'm told what my opinion is on certain things. Every time Celtic has a win I get: "You'll have been celebrating the other night, eh?" I can't *stand* football, and my Tommy supports Partick Thistle. Many's the time I've felt like letting the hot tongs slip against a bare neck.'

'Let them say what they like,' Joe's granny chipped in. 'It's what they used to do that was worse. Open discrimination. It's not so long ago that building sites had signs up: NO IRISH NEED APPLY. The London *Times* carried adverts for maids that said: NO CATHOLICS.'

'Those days are gone, Mother,' Joe had heard his dad say. 'We shouldn't live in the past.'

'It's all very well for you to say that, Joseph. Remember, it wasn't my past. It was my present.'

'It's the past now,' his dad insisted.

'Is it?' his mother asked.

When Joe's granny's family had parties or family get-togethers they often told stories. Lots were funny family stories, like his granny's first encounter with certain attitudes in Glasgow. When she'd come over from Ireland as a young married woman she'd lived in a tenement in the Tollcross area. She'd been hanging out her washing one day and saw, across the back court, another woman from the next close doing the same thing. Joe's granny told the story of how she thought she'd be friendly and went over and introduced herself.

' "I'm Brigid Flaherty," I said.

' "Hah!" this woman cried at once. "I knew it! You're a Catholic, aren't you?"

'I laughed and said, "I suppose it's my name and the Irish accent."

' "Och," she said, "I could tell you were a Pape before you even opened your mouth."

' "How did you manage that?" I asked her.

' "I was standing here watching you hinging your washing out, hen. You Irish Catholics peg the trousers up a different way from us Prods." '

Joe's granny wiped tears of laughter from her eyes. 'Would you believe that?' she said. 'In Scotland there's a Catholic and a Protestant way to hang up your drawers. Mind you,' she added, 'her and I became good friends. She was the first one knocking on my door to help out when I was having my bairns.'

Other times, at Joe's family get-togethers, it was old, old history that was taken out and relived. The Famine – when millions of Irish died or were forced to emigrate. The suppression and slaughter of the Irish people – like the massacre at Drogheda. Cromwell was responsible for that. Oliver Cromwell. He'd dispossessed them, driven them from their own fertile land, out to the wild wastes of the western province of Ireland. He'd ordered them to make their choice. '*To Hell or Connaught.*' No choice. They'd been banished to that part of Ireland that could support neither man nor beast. And they'd to smash boulders to try to farm the poor soil. 'Sure the very sheep broke their teeth on the rocks,' Joe heard his granny say on one occasion.

He had been quite small at the time, playing at the feet of the adults in his granny's house. A picture had instantly formed in his head. A sheep with false teeth. Joe laughed. Because he could see it right there, standing in a field. A goofy-looking sheep, grinning, with great big false teeth. He laughed again. Suddenly he knew that he was very loud. The adults had fallen silent. He looked up. He saw that he was the only one laughing.

No one else joined in.

Joe had been very very young when he realized that, in his family, stories like that were not funny.

Chapter 5

'This yin's in a bad way.'

The first paramedic out of the ambulance in Reglan Street waved her arm to the driver. 'Back up. Get the stretcher. Let's move!'

'What happened?' she asked Graham.

'A gang of boys jumped him. One of them had a knife.'

'He can't be more than eighteen,' the woman said as she examined him. 'Just a kid.'

'I'll go,' said Graham. He tried to disentangle himself from Kyoul's grasp.

'Naw, son. You keep a hold of his hand there. It might be the only thing connecting him to us.'

Graham looked down to where Kyoul was holding his hand. He saw that blood from the older boy's wound had seeped onto the sleeve of his school sweatshirt.

As they neared the hospital Kyoul drifted into consciousness. His eyes opened, recognized Graham. He smiled sadly. 'Thank you for staying with me.'

There was a doctor and two nurses waiting as the

ambulance pulled up, siren screaming, at the City Hospital Accident and Emergency. The driver jumped out of the cab to help transfer Kyoul to the waiting trolley. When the stretcher was safely out of the ambulance the paramedic inside spoke to Graham.

'Your friend needs to go to theatre immediately.' She picked up Graham's bag. 'Come on,' she said kindly. 'I'll show you where you can wait while he's being taken care of.'

QUIET WAITING ROOM.

Graham read the sign. There was a woman sitting in the room already. She sat straight-backed, staring ahead. Tears streaked her face. When Graham came in she patted her eyes with a tissue and tried to smile at him.

Graham slumped into a chair near the door. This was a disaster. Why had he stupidly said to the paramedic that he'd seen the gang of boys? She'd mentioned before she left him that someone would come and speak to him soon. They would ask questions, telephone his parents. He would have to explain why he was going via Reglan Street instead of leaving the sports grounds the proper way and going home via the main road. It wouldn't take his parents long to work out he'd taken a dodgy short cut so that he could spend most of his bus fare on chips and chocolate. How was it that half an hour ago things had been going fine, and now he was in more bother than he could handle? If his mum and dad had to come and collect him from the hospital it would cause the most tremendous amount of trouble. He was always complaining that they were overprotective and it was only recently that he'd been allowed to go places on his own. If they discovered he hadn't been totally straight with them then they might not let him visit his Granda Reid tomorrow, like he did every Saturday, to go with him to Ibrox Park to watch Rangers play. If they found out he'd taken that short cut every week they wouldn't allow him to compete in the rest of the football trials. There would be no more football matches of any description – not to play in, not to watch, not to talk about even. No football whatever. He was doomed.

Graham glanced at his watch. He had less than thirty minutes to get home before they would start to worry. He checked his watch again. If – if he could get away right now . . . Graham reckoned he had enough time to get home without being too late. This hospital was closer to his side of the city so the ambulance had actually taken him a good bit of the way home already. He couldn't help Kyoul by staying here. In fact it would only make things worse. Whoever came to speak to him might look in his bag and find Kyoul's phone. They'd read the note in his notebook with Kyoul's girlfriend's address, contact her, and then her parents would find out. Or supposing it was the police? They'd call his parents or they might even take him home in a police car! If only he could slip out unnoticed . . .

Graham stood up.

The woman with the tear-streaked face spoke to him. 'Are you all right, son? My man's had a heart attack. The waiting's terrible, isn't it? Is nobody with you?'

'Yes,' said Graham quickly, 'my mum's on her way. But I – I . . .'

'The toilet? D'you need the toilet?'

'No. Yes.' Graham nodded.

The woman went to the door with him. 'See how you came in through the main waiting area? Go that way and it's the door in front of you.'

Graham hung back.

'You don't want to go through Accident and Emergency? Don't blame you. It's getting like a zoo out there. I don't know how the staff put up with it. There's a toilet in the main part of the hospital. Go to the end of this corridor, turn left, and you'll see the sign.'

Graham went into the corridor leading away from A&E towards the main exit. Evening visiting was finishing. Eyes on the ground, he mingled with the crowd and walked out through the front doors of the hospital.

Once outside the gate he pulled off his bloodied sweatshirt, rolled it up and stuffed it to the bottom of his rucksack.

Chapter 6

When Joe had finished clearing up in his granny's hairdressing shop he caught a bus that would take him to his part of the city.

Getting off at the stop before his own, he ran up the path of his granny's house and put the shop keys through her letter box. After he'd done that he walked the short distance to his home. He wondered what state his dad would be in tonight. Before he'd gone to school that morning Joe had written out a number of things for his dad to do. 'Keep him busy' – that was the advice everyone gave. Sometimes his dad managed all the tasks on the list – get dressed, wash dishes, tidy up, etc. More usually half the stuff got done half well.

Often Joe could tell even before he opened the front door whether his dad was having a good day or bad day. He turned the corner into his own street. From here he could see his house silhouetted against the darkening sky. All the lights were off.

Joe heaved a sigh.

It had been a bad day then.

* * *

When Graham arrived home his parents were in the kitchen putting away groceries from their weekly Friday evening shop. He said hello as he came through the back door, slid past them and went up to his room. He took his school sweatshirt from his rucksack, put it in a plastic carrier and lobbed it onto the top of his wardrobe. Tomorrow he'd get rid of it on the way to his granda's house. He had three or four school sweatshirts. If his mum noticed that one was missing he'd tell her that he'd lost it somewhere.

Graham knew that one of his parents would call him for his supper quite soon but he'd enough time to check something out. He sat at his desk, switched on his computer and logged on. He got to the Internet site he was looking for – maps4u.co.uk – and found the address Kyoul had written out. It wasn't easy to read but he could make out 'Merchant City', and he recalled Kyoul saying that his girlfriend Leanne lived in the High Street. Graham entered *Merchant City, Glasgow* in the search box and zoomed into the High Street. It was a continuation of Castle Street, curving from the direction of the M8 motorway down to the Tollbooth Steeple and Glasgow Cross. He didn't know how the buildings were numbered, but Merchant City was clearly marked, and Kyoul had written down the house number. Also it wasn't too far away from Bridgebar, the part of Glasgow where his Granda Reid lived. Graham reasoned there was no harm in going there tomorrow, on his way to his granda's, to look for the house. He knew the landmarks round that area. It was the historical centre of the city. He'd been on a school trip there not so long ago. He remembered a visit to Provand's Lordship, the oldest house in Glasgow, and trailing round the Cathedral before going into the St Mungo Museum of Religion. And Granda Reid, who was an Orangeman, took him every year to see the statue of William of Orange, King Billy, which stood close by the little cobbled square. Graham hadn't decided if he would definitely deliver Kyoul's message and return the phone – he would see if he could find the house and then make up his mind. He printed the page and, on an impulse, keyed *asylum seekers* into a search engine.

There were thousands of hits. Graham checked out a few and then some related websites. There was loads of information on asylum seekers. It came to him that he had no idea about some of things that were happening in the world. He didn't often watch news programmes and, although his parents contributed to Children in Need, he hadn't really thought of the suffering of others that much. He clicked the images on the website of Médecins Sans Frontières, an organization that provided aid all over the globe, and finally reached the pages for the various Refugee Councils. Graham opened a box marked *Rumours & Realities* and began to read the entries.

The door of his room opened and his mum came in. 'Schoolwork?' She looked over his shoulder.

'Uh,' said Graham.

'Asylum seekers? It's a complex problem.' His mum leaned over to see better. 'You might be interested to know that one of the lawyers I work for is dealing with a victim compensation case. Two Kurds were set upon in the street in Glasgow. It happened when the first British soldiers were killed in the Iraq war. The men who did it knew their victims were from Iraq and thought this was a way of avenging the soldiers' deaths. But they were so ignorant that they didn't realize that the Kurdish race suffered horribly under Saddam Hussein and that they were actually attacking refugees. Awful, isn't it? To think that these Kurds come here for safety, and are beaten up by the very people they think will protect them against brutality.'

'It says here that eighty per cent of asylum seekers in Glasgow who have had a decision on their case are genuinely escaping oppression,' said Graham.

'I know,' said his mum. 'Most of them arrive and get on with their lives. But that doesn't make the news. The media go after the big success story or else focus on the very negative. Some of the newspapers print inflammatory statements, like claiming Britain is being swamped, but we're not. In fact, here's a statistic that'll interest you. If we put all our asylum seekers into the national stadium at Hampden Park they wouldn't come close to filling it.'

She touched Graham lightly on the shoulder. 'Supper's ready when you are.'

Graham waited till his mum left and then logged off. He stood up and collected the map printout. He folded it carefully and put it with Kyoul's letter in the pocket of the jacket he would wear tomorrow. It should be easy to get away in the early morning. Both his parents went out every Saturday, his dad to play golf while his mum went through to Edinburgh to shop and lunch with friends.

Usually Graham lay in bed on a Saturday morning until it was time for him to visit his Granda Reid. Tomorrow he'd be ready to go as soon as his mum and dad left.

Chapter 7

YOU ARE NOW ENTERING FREE GARNGATH.

Graham's stomach cramped as he caught sight of the words spray-painted on the gable end of the building directly in front of him.

He was lost. Dangerously lost.

This morning had started well. His parents had gone off first thing. He'd mumbled a sleepy 'bye' to them from under his duvet. When he heard their cars draw away he'd leaped up, grabbed a roll and a packet of crisps and run to catch a bus to the city centre. It was a bright morning, a great day for this afternoon's football match. Sitting on the bus, Graham ate his food and felt more relaxed than he'd been last night. 'Things always look better in the morning' was one of his Granda Reid's say-ings, and he was right. The bus was making good speed, leaving behind his familiar streets of detached and semi-detached houses, travelling swiftly into more built-up districts. Graham took the street map from his pocket. The city centre was only a couple of stops away now. He figured he could do this easily. He shouldn't have got so strung out last night. Kyoul should recover and delivering the message and returning the mobile for him would be quite straightforward. The carrier bag containing the bloodied sweatshirt lay on the seat beside him. Graham was pleased that he'd remembered to bring it with him to dump it somewhere. He began to plan how he might spend the money that Kyoul had promised would be his. Then from the bus window he saw a skip next to a building site. That would do. He would sling it in there. By the end of the day it would be covered in rubble.

Graham got off the bus, ran across the road and threw the bag up and into the skip. Perfect. He'd less than a mile to walk and he'd be at the High Street. He jogged after the bus . . . and pulled up short at the next bend. He'd forgotten the motorway! The infamous M8 that bisected the city. The one his dad moaned about. 'Most cities build their ring road round *outside* the centre – that's why they're known as ring roads. But not Glasgow. Oh no. We have to do it in reverse. We run ours right through the middle of the town.'

Graham had watched the bus disappearing along the slip road and looked at his map again. He'd have to make a massive detour. He'd started walking, then spotted a pedestrian bridge a short distance away. It crossed the motorway connecting the north side of the city to the centre. Graham had taken what he thought was the most direct way to get to it.

And stumbled into the Garngath.

Nobody in their right mind came up here.

It was where the die-hard Celtic-supporting Tims all

lived. For a true-blue Rangers fan he was in the worst place he could be.

He had entered marked-out territory.

Green scarves, banners and flags were hanging from windows and railings. Graham turned his head. There was anti-Rangers stuff sprayed on the opposite wall:

NO HUNS.
NO BILLY BOYS.

The city always cleaned off this type of graffiti as fast as possible, but on the day of Rangers v Celtic games it reappeared in certain areas. Graham knew that by now the walls in and around Bridgebar would have their own slogans painted across them. On the day of an Old Firm derby some of those streets were swathed in Rangers colours, with occasionally even the kerbstones coloured red, white and blue. Up here in the Garngath the place was festooned in green and white.

At this time of the day there weren't many people on the streets or in their gardens. A man approached, walking his dog. Should he ask him for directions? Supposing the man caught sight of the Rangers club scarf tucked under his jacket? Anything could happen. It wasn't so long ago that a Celtic supporter had been attacked when he'd gone into the wrong pub wearing his colours. The dog stopped to sniff at Graham's legs, wagged its tail and looked up to be patted. Graham backed away.

'He'll no touch you, son,' said the man. 'He's just being friendly.'

Graham gave the dog and the man a weak smile and crossed the road. He needed to find a quiet place with no one watching him where he could take out the map printout and have a good look at it. There was a building up ahead with a yard attached. As he got nearer he saw that it was a school. The sign on the wall read ST VERONICA'S. It was the school of the boy from the football trials. A Roman Catholic school. It looked much the same as Graham's own school. Maybe he could slip in through the gate, find somewhere out of sight in the playground to study his map. But the gates were closed and locked. Graham walked on a bit further. A group of men on the corner called over to him.

'C'mere, son,' one of them shouted. 'I want you to go a message for me.'

Graham shook his head and hurried on. Tricolours and bunting stretched across the next street. He seemed to be going deeper into enemy territory.

'Hey, you!'

Graham turned his head.

'Aye. *You!*' An older boy had appeared behind him. 'What are you doing here?'

'What's it to you?' countered Graham. His heart began to beat faster.

'What school do you go to?'

'None of your business.'

The boy took in Graham's face and his clothes. 'You don't belong here.'

'Aye I do,' said Graham shortly, and tried to walk away.

The older boy grabbed his sleeve. 'I don't like

the look of you,' he snarled. 'You've got a Protestant face.'

'What does that mean?' Graham said. 'A *Protestant* face?'

'I can tell.' The older boy shoved his own face up against Graham's. 'Your wee beady eyes are too close together.'

Graham opened his eyes as wide as he could and tried to laugh it off, but he was taken aback. It hadn't occurred to him that Catholics might think that Protestants looked different from them. His knew that some Protestants regarded Catholics as a separate race. He hadn't realized it worked the other way. His Uncle Maxwell believed absolutely that Catholics had definite physical characteristics that were not the same as Protestants'. Graham had heard him say it often enough, especially at the New Year, when his uncle had too much drink in him. 'They're a different breed, the Tims. I'm telling you. In a way I feel sorry for them. 'Cos the thing with the Cathlicks is, they cannae help being taken in by aw that mumbo-jumbo their priests tell them. It's because they're mair stupit than us, see? Their brains are actually *smaller*. Inside their skulls, like. Naw, naw, listen,' he protested as people began to laugh. 'Listen. Don't take my word for it. It's been proven. Away and read it for yoursel. Check in any of them big medical books. It's a scientific fact, so it is.'

Graham looked at the boy challenging him. If anything, this boy's head was considerably bigger than Graham's own.

'You're a Hun,' the boy said, blocking the pavement.

'Naw,' said Graham, trying to tough it out.

'I'm gonna give you a kicking anyway,' the older boy decided.

'I'm here to see my pal,' said Graham, and tried to push his way past.

'Who's that then?'

'Joseph,' said Graham desperately, remembering the name of the boy from St Veronica's who had set up the goal for him at the football practice the previous evening. 'Joe Flaherty.' He spoke up more boldly. 'I'm here to meet Joe Flaherty.'

'Well, you're in luck,' said the older boy, taking Graham's arm and bending it up his back. 'He's my cousin. So I'll just take you right to his front door then.'

Chapter 8

'This yin says he knows your Joe.'

'What?'

The man looking down at Graham from his doorstep was dressed in trousers and a pyjama top.

'Your Joe, Uncle Joseph. This yin says he's his pal.'

'Does he?' The man, who Graham guessed was Joe Flaherty's father, peered uncertainly at Graham. He shook his head. 'I've never seen him before.'

'Knew it!' the older boy declared triumphantly. He gave Graham a hard punch on the shoulder. 'Lying wee nyaff.'

'Haud on. Haud on, Jammy.' The man waved his hand at the older boy. 'Maybe he *is* a pal of Joe's.'

'I met Joseph at football training, Mr Flaherty. We played together last night.' Graham spoke up as clearly and confidently as he could.

'*I met Joseph at the football training, Mr Flaherty.*' The boy mimicked Graham's accent in a high, squeaky voice. '*We played together last night.*'

Graham's face flushed scarlet. He tried to pull away, but the other boy's grip tightened. 'Maybe Joe told you about it,' Graham said quickly to Joe's father, who was looking vaguer by the second.

'See the way he speaks, even?' The boy holding Graham addressed Joe's dad. 'He's no one of us. You can tell.'

'It was Joe that set up the goal that I scored at the end of last night's match,' Graham gabbled on. 'Brilliant player, Joe. He is.'

'We don't need the likes of you to tell us that Joe can play football.' The older boy shook Graham's shoulder. 'Do we, Uncle Joseph? We know that for ourselves. Don't we, Uncle Joseph? And if anybody was scoring a goal it would be Joe, not you. Wouldn't it, Uncle Joseph?'

'Aye. Aye. Aye. Aye.' Joe's father put his hand to his forehead. 'You're giving me a headache, Jammy.'

'Sorry, Uncle Joseph. I'll take this yin away and thump his face for him.'

'Mr Flaherty!' Graham cried out. 'Is Joe anywhere about?'

'Joe's in his room.' Joe's dad glanced towards the staircase. 'Listening to music with his headset on, no doubt. JOE!' He raised his voice. 'JOE! CAN YOU COME HERE A MINUTE PLEASE!'

'What is it?'

To Graham's relief Joe appeared at the top of the stairs, earphones trailing round his shoulder.

'There's someone here says he knows you,' Joe's dad told him. 'Jammy's appointed himself on guard duty 'cos we're playing the Sons of William today. Your cousin's secured the perimeter, and already made a citizen's arrest. "*Ils ne passeront pas*" and all that.' Joe's dad laughed as he made his way slowly through to the living room.

Joe came down the stairs. 'What's going on?'

'This yin . . .' With his free hand Joe's cousin cuffed Graham across the head. 'This yin claims he plays football with you.'

'Yeh?' Joe frowned at Graham. Then his face altered in recognition. 'Aye, so he does.'

'Oh.' The older boy let go Graham's arm. 'He was acting funny when I saw him. What I'd like to know is, what's a Hun doing up here in the Garngath, today of all days?'

'What are you talking about, Jammy?' said Joe, grabbing Graham and hauling him across the doorstep.

'He's no right to be here. He's a Hun.'

'Sez who?' Joe challenged the older boy.

'I can tell.'

'Ach, away you go.' Joe laughed.

'I'll come in and make sure you're OK,' offered Jammy, making to enter the house.

'Gie's peace, Jammy.' Joe pushed his cousin off the front doorstep and closed the door. 'C'mon up the stair,' he said to Graham.

'Your cousin was going to give me a doing.' Graham found that his voice was not quite steady.

'Naw,' said Joe. 'He didn't mean it.'

'I believed him.'

'He's half daft,' Joe explained. 'All talk, Jammy is.'

'Is that his name?' Graham asked. 'Is he really called Jammy?'

'Well, his ma, my Aunt Rita, christened him Sammy when he was born, but he had this accident when he was a baby. Fell on his head, like. Tumbled out his pram. Cracked his skull on the pavement. They rushed him into the Royal. Thought he was a goner. Ambulance man said he wouldn't make it, but he did. The doctor at the hospital told his ma that they were amazed he'd even woken up again.' Joe put on a posh voice. '*Your son, Mrs Flaherty, has survived a terrible trauma. He is indeed a very fortunate little fellow.* My Aunt Rita told the story when she got home. *See oor Sammy?* she said. *Mair like jammy, I'd say. Jammy wee b, so he is.* The name stuck. After that everyone called him Jammy. He's lucky to be alive.

'Mind you,' Joe added, as he paused outside his bedroom door, 'he's been no right in the heid ever since.'

Chapter 9

Joe opened the door of his bedroom and Graham stepped into a green grotto.

Every inch of wall, floor and ceiling was green and white. Carpet, curtains, rug, bedcover, reading lamp, wallpaper, lampshade and all the paintwork were the same colours. Posters of Celtic footballers past and present were pinned on the walls, the ceiling and the wardrobe. The very door handle, Graham noticed as Joe closed the door behind him, was a green-and-white football.

'Sit down,' said Joe, pointing to a green-and-white striped chair in front of a matching desk.

Graham gulped. There was nowhere he could put himself that part of his body would not be touching some of the despised and hated Celtic paraphernalia. His Granda Reid would have a heart attack.

'I'll stand,' he said.

'Suit yourself.' Joe flung himself on his bed, tipping some Celtic magazines onto the floor at Graham's feet.

Graham stepped back.

'What did you want to see me for?' Joe asked.

'Em . . .' Graham swallowed.

'It's quite a way for you to come up here,' said Joe. 'Don't you live out in Robrostoun?'

'Yes.' Graham swallowed again.

'And are you no going to the game the day?'

'Aye.'

Joe was suddenly aware that Graham's jacket was buttoned to the neck on what was quite a warm morning.

'Have you got your colours on underneath that jacket?'

Graham nodded.

'Jeeeeeez,' said Joe. He shook his head. 'No wonder you looked feart when Jammy brought you to the door.' He used one of his granny's expressions: 'Have you lost your mind? Or are you just lost?' As he said the words something clicked in Joe's head. 'You *are* lost, aren't you?'

Graham nodded again.

'How did you land up here?'

'I wanted to get across the motorway and took a wrong turning.' Graham made a face. 'More than one. I was trying to work out which direction to go when I saw the name St Veronica on the side of a building. I remembered that was the school you went to. Then your cousin stopped me in the street and challenged me. I thought you might live somewhere here. I had to say something. He was going to batter me.'

'But what were you doing in this area in the first place?' Joe asked. 'Going somewhere you didn't know you were going?'

'I had a message to deliver.'

Joe laughed. 'Did you no think to put a stamp on it and shove it in a postbox?'

'It's more complicated than that.' Graham took the piece of paper torn from his school notebook and showed it to Joe. He told Joe most of what had happened the previous evening.

'You were lucky that gang didn't do for you an all,' said Joe. 'Headbangers like that? They'd knife anybody.'

'I know,' said Graham. 'I was terrified. When they ran off I thought Kyoul was dead. The paramedics said that probably I saved his life by calling the ambulance. When Kyoul told me his story I suppose I felt kind of obliged to let his girlfriend know where he is.'

Joe shook his head. 'It doesn't explain why you ended up in the Garngath.'

'I got off the bus too early. And I was trying to work out a way to get across the motorway. Then your cousin grabbed me.'

'Let me see.' Joe scrutinized the map. 'This is the page for the Merchant City area that you've got here.'

'Yes,' said Graham. He sat on the very edge of the bed.

Joe picked up the letter again. 'But that's not Merchant City that's written on the last line of the address.'

Graham leaned over Joe's shoulder. 'It is. Look.' He spelled out the letters, 'M-E-R-C-H-A-N-T. And the second word is *City*.'

'The letters are all uneven,' said Joe, 'and the first word does look like *Merchant* but I don't think the second one says *City*.'

Graham recalled that last night in the street Kyoul

could barely hold the pencil in his hand. 'What does it say then?'

'He's scrawled it out so that it's got a gap between the first part and the second, but I think it's all one word.' Joe squinted at the writing again. 'It's Merchantstown,' he said at last.

'Merchantstown?' said Graham.

'Yes,' said Joe. 'Where the rich people live. A completely different side of the city from this.'

'But Kyoul said his girlfriend lived in the High Street, and the High Street runs between Castle Street and the Trongate. That bit of Glasgow is known as the Merchant City. It's on my map page that's marked "Merchant City".'

'There must be more than one High Street in Glasgow then,' said Joe. 'You should have checked the phone book.'

'I don't know her second name.'

'Well it looks like he's written "Merchantstown" to me.'

Graham looked at the letter again. 'I think you're right,' he said. 'And it makes more sense. Kyoul said she lived in a house with a big garden. There's only flats in the city centre.' He knocked on his own forehead with his knuckles. 'How could I have been so stupid not to realize that?'

Joe shrugged. 'It sounded familiar so you probably thought of the first street you knew.'

'That means I'd need to take this letter all the way across the river and I don't know that part of the city.'

'Throw it the bin then,' said Joe.

'I can't,' said Graham.

'Why not?'

'I told you, I feel I ought to deliver it. He's in a bad way, she doesn't know what's happened to him, and . . .'

'And?'

'Well . . . he told me the girl would give me money for bringing the phone back to her.'

'Give you money?' said Joe suspiciously.

'Fifty quid,' said Graham. 'Kyoul said she was well off. He said he'd put it in the letter asking her. He wanted me to take her mobile phone directly to her and tell her what happened to him as early as I could this morning. It would be like claiming a reward.'

'Sounds like drugs,' said Joe. 'You don't want anything to do with that.'

'No,' said Graham. 'He swore it wasn't anything to do with drugs. And I think he was telling the truth.'

'Still sounds dodgy to me.'

'He said they were in love, but her family wouldn't approve. Like Romeo and Juliet, I suppose. You know about Romeo and Juliet?'

'I know fine,' said Joe. 'It's a play where everybody ends up dead.'

There was a silence in the room.

Then Joe said, 'What're you going to do?'

Graham consulted his watch. 'I usually visit my granda in Bridgebar on a Saturday. We're going to the game together today. It's at Parkhead.'

'I know that,' said Joe. 'I'm going with my da.'

'Well it's your ground, so my granda likes to go early. He always does that when Rangers are playing there – to avoid any trouble. So even though I'd like to take the phone back to this girl because I promised I would, I don't think I've got enough time to get all the way to the south side and back again.'

'You've got enough time,' said Joe. 'Just about.'

'How do you know?'

'One of my uncles lives over there. I go and see my cousins sometimes.'

They looked at each other.

'If you came with me I'd split the money,' said Graham.

Joe stared at him.

'Halfers,' said Graham.

Joe didn't take long to think it over. 'You're on,' he said, and stood up. 'But first I need to fix up my dad.'

Chapter 10

Graham wondered what Joe had to do to 'fix up' his dad so that he could leave the house.

His own parents were pretty protective but even they allowed him out on a Saturday morning. 'Does your dad watch what you're doing all the time?' he asked Joe.

'More the opposite,' said Joe. He lifted a savings bank (green and white) from his desk and took out some money. 'He'll be sitting about waiting for the run-up to the match on the telly, but he probably hasn't eaten any breakfast. C'mon.'

Once downstairs Joe pulled open his front door. 'I have to find Jammy,' he told Graham.

'Oh no,' said Graham.

'Believe me, I would rather avoid him too, but at this moment we need him. Otherwise we won't have enough time to see to my dad and get across the city.' Joe stood on his front doorstep. 'JAMMY!' he roared at the top of his voice. 'JAMMY!'

Graham looked out nervously. Bunting idled in the morning air. Apart from that, no movement.

Joe walked to the front gate. 'JAMMY! Where are you? C'mon. I need you. JAMMY!'

Graham stepped back as he saw Jammy loping up the street.

'I knew you'd want my help with that yin,' Graham heard Jammy say as he came into the garden with Joe. 'Want me to lamp him now?'

'Enough,' Joe told his cousin. 'He's good. He's a pal of mine.'

'What's your name then?' Jammy came forward and inspected Graham.

'Gra—'

'Gregory,' Joe cut in. 'His name's Gregory. After a pope. See?'

'What?' said Graham.

Joe whacked Graham in the ribs. 'Your mammy called you after a pope. Isn't that right, *Gregory*?'

'A pope?' said Graham.

'A pope?' repeated Jammy. The scowl left his face. 'So he's no a Hun?'

'You're catching on, Jammy,' said Joe. 'You're a smart one the day.'

Jammy's face broke into a big grin. 'A pope?' he said again. 'It's no often you get a pope up here in the Garngath.'

'I do not believe this,' said Graham under his breath.

'I want you to do something for me, Jammy,' said Joe.

'Anything,' said Jammy. 'You and me are pals, aren't we, Joe?'

'Sure are,' said Joe.

'Best pals?'

'The very best. Listen, Jammy, will you?'

'I'm listening. I'm listening.'

'I want you go to Abdul's and get us some stuff for my dad. Say it's for Mr Flaherty and Abdul will know that you've to get rolls and milk and the papers. OK?'

'OK.' Jammy nodded enthusiastically. 'OK.'

'What are you going for?' Joe asked him.

'Rolls and milk and the papers,' Jammy repeated. 'Rolls and milk and the papers.'

'That's great. You've got it, Jammy.' Joe put the money in his cousin's jacket pocket. 'Don't take that out till you get to the shop.'

'I won't. I won't,' said Jammy. He ran off happily as the boys went into the house.

'Dad?'

Joe's dad was sitting in the living room staring into space. He gave a start as Joe spoke.

'What, son? What?'

'Go and finish getting dressed.' Joe spoke firmly to his father. 'I've sent Jammy for the rolls and your papers. I'll make you some tea. Go on,' he said more gently. 'I've got to go out this morning and I want to see you put a shirt on and eat something before I go.'

'You're coming back though?'

'Aye. Aye. Don't worry. I'll be here in time to take you to the game.'

While Joe and his dad were talking, Graham glanced around the room. It was smaller than the lounge in his own house but nicely furnished in shades of cream and brown. On the mantelpiece above the fireplace was a photograph of a woman and . . . a small wooden crucifix.

'There's always a sign.' Graham could hear his Granda Reid's voice in his head. *'You can always tell. Even nowadays, when a lot of them don't bother with holy pictures hanging up and statues to this yin and that yin. But if you're in any of their houses, look about you. You'll see a wee icon or somethin. Idolatry. That's what it is.'*

'C'mon.' Joe tugged Graham's sleeve and Graham followed him into the kitchen. 'Help yourself to some juice from the fridge.'

Working at speed, Joe put the kettle on, rinsed last night's dishes in the sink, set out some plates, cut half a dozen slices of cheese and made a pot of tea before Jammy was battering once again on the door.

'Got the rolls and the milk and the papers.' Jammy nodded cheerfully at Graham. He put them on the table and handed over the change to Joe. 'Mr Abdul says hello.'

'You done well, Jammy,' said Joe. 'The boy done good. Didn't he, Gra— Gregory?'

'What? Oh yeh. Yeh.'

Jammy beamed at both of them.

'You done brilliant,' said Joe. He gave Jammy a few coins. 'Away and buy yourself some sweeties. And Jammy,' he shouted after his cousin, 'stay out of trouble today.

'It's a good job Jammy doesn't have a ticket for the game this afternoon,' Joe said as his dad, now fully dressed with hair combed, came into the kitchen and sat at the table. 'One of these days someone's going to do him.'

'Aye' – Joe's dad picked up the teapot – 'and it might no be somebody from the other side that does it.'

'Right, Dad.' Joe plonked the bundle of newspapers on the table in front of his father. 'You've to have that *Guardian* crossword done by the time I get back.'

'Can your dad do the *Guardian* crossword?' Graham asked as the two boys left the house.

'It's a joke between us,' said Joe.

'Uh-huh.' Graham laughed. 'I thought that.'

'Did you?' Joe turned his head and gave Graham a long look. 'Actually, my dad *can* do the *Guardian* crossword.'

Chapter 11

'D'you know what bus we need to get to the south side and where to get off?'

Graham was jogging to keep up with Joe.

'Not exactly,' said Joe. 'But I know where to find out. We'll go to the Mungo Museum. My dad's cousin works in there. He'll let us see a map of Glasgow and we'll find out exactly where we're going.'

They walked together onto the pedestrian bridge that spanned the M8 and led to the city centre. Gorse and broom blazed gold on the grass-verged side of the motorway and in the distance the blue-hazed hills swelled against the horizon.

'You can see a lot from up here,' said Graham, pausing in the middle.

'Yeh. It's the highest point in the city,' said Joe. 'Brilliant place to live, the Garngath.'

Graham looked at him to see if he was joking. 'Aye, right.'

Joe's eyes narrowed but he said nothing, only continued walking across the bridge and down the steps leading to Alexandra Parade. The two boys came onto the curve of Castle Street and past the Royal Infirmary, looking like Hogwarts, with its fascinating dark turrets and towers. Before them the High Street straightened out for its descent towards Glasgow Cross. On the right was the ancient hospital of the monks and on their left, set back from the road, the old cathedral. They crossed the square with its lampposts showing the curled coat of arms of the city – the Bell, the Fish, the Bird and the Tree – to the St Mungo Museum of Religious Life and Art.

Joe swung the glass door open and they went inside. 'Upstairs,' he said. 'That's where the information desk is.' He took the stairs two at a time.

Within seconds a uniformed attendant was on their heels.

'We're going to get bounced,' Graham told him out of the side of his mouth.

'Naw.' Joe turned and grinned at the security guard. 'Hi, Pat,' he said. 'I need to find out what bus to get to the High Street on the south side.'

'Oh, it's you, Joe.' The guard smiled in recognition. 'Sure, hang on and I'll get a transport map from behind the desk.'

Graham looked around as they waited at the top of the stairs. It was a couple of years since he'd been here with his school. Through the archway he could see what his teacher had called Glasgow's most famous piece of art: Salvador Dali's painting of Christ of St John of the Cross. Graham remembered the museum guide raving on about how beautiful it was – this unusual, dramatic view of Jesus Christ stretched on his cross. The figure was suspended over some men and fishing boats beside a peaceful seashore. Depicted from high above, it showed a man, head bowed, with no sign of wounds or struggle upon his body. And though Graham was intrigued, like the rest of his class, to find the outline of the dove enclosed within the muscle of the upper arm, he much preferred the hands-on room upstairs. He'd enjoyed the quizzes on the different religions, doing the games and the brass rubbings, and looking at the prayer mats, one with a built-in compass to enable the user to find the direction of the Kaaba in Mecca.

Joe saw where Graham was looking and pointed to the huge painting. 'You know, visitors come from all over the world to see that image.'

Graham shivered.

'What's the matter?' said Joe.

'I don't like it.'

'You're in the minority then,' said Joe. 'It's part of Glasgow. Though my dad thinks it was better where it was before they moved it here. It was in the Kelvingrove. He says people queued for hours to see it when it first arrived.'

'Know a lot about painting, does he, your dad?'

Joe waited a moment before replying, unsure if Graham was being sarcastic, then said, 'He knows a lot about everything, my dad.'

'Here you go.' Joe's cousin Pat had returned with the map. As he unfolded it he asked Joe, 'How's your dad, by the way?'

'Up and down,' said Joe.

Pat shook his head. 'It's a terrible thing, thon depression.'

Depression. That was it! Graham now knew what had

struck him as being familiar about Joe's dad. It was the way he held himself, the way he looked. It was the same way his Aunt Kirsty looked when she'd got depression after the birth of her baby. Graham thought of Joe's dad again, the flat expression in his eyes.

'You say to him to come over to us for dinner,' Pat told Joe. 'Any night. He's a fine man, your da. Your ma was that proud of him.'

'I know. Everybody says that.'

'Tell him, mind now.'

'I'll tell him, Pat. I'll tell him.'

'I've found the place you're looking for.' Pat pointed to a street on the other side of the river. 'It's a street over in Merchantstown, just off the main road. You can get a bus to it from here. There's a bus stop nearby. If you walk outside and turn left in the direction of the Tollbooth, it's only a yard or so.'

Pat showed them where the other High Street was located on the south side of the city and told them the number of the bus to take.

As he saw them to the door he said to Joe, 'You'll be going to the game this afternoon with your dad?'

'Oh aye,' said Joe.

'We'll hammer the Huns today for sure.'

'Oh aye,' said Joe.

'*Oh aye*,' Graham mimicked Joe once they were away from the doorway and out of earshot. 'Hammer the Huns? If you're referring to the mighty Glasgow Rangers, who have players like Houston and McMahon, the best in Scotland, I *don't* think so. Not with that bunch of losers you call a team.'

'Ha!' Joe scoffed in return. 'Wait till you see our *bhoys* in action. Kerr and Carmichael are going to kick your erchies from here to kingdom come.'

'Carmichael's keech,' sneered Graham.

'Is not,' said Joe. He lunged at Graham, who jumped away laughing.

They dodged through a group of tourists photographing the statue in a little grass enclosure beyond the museum.

'Take a photograph of anything, they would,' said Joe.

'That's not just anyone,' said Graham. He gave Joe a sidelong glance. 'Very important person, King Billy.'

'King Billy!' Joe turned to look at the statue of a man dressed as a Roman emperor. 'That's *never* King Billy. We don't have a statue to King Billy in the middle of our city!'

'Aye we do,' said Graham. 'Read the inscription.'

'There's our bus,' said Joe. 'C'mon, we'll need to run.'

Graham felt better as they sat on the top deck of the bus on the way across the city. Mr Joe Know-it-all didn't know so much after all. Graham's granda took him to see that statue every year at the beginning of July before setting off to Northern Ireland for the celebrations in Ulster on the twelfth. The Orange Walk was the biggest event in his granda's life. Granda Reid had been a member of his local Orange Lodge since he was a young man. And William of Orange, King Billy, was his big hero. He was made King when Parliament turned against King James and deposed him after he became a Catholic. King James tried to retake his throne by coming through Ireland like a back door, and he used the native Irish Catholics in his army. Most of the Protestants sided with King Billy and, north of Dublin, they beat back James's army at the Battle of the Boyne on the twelfth of July in 1690. Granda Reid told Graham that the statue used to stand near the Trongate, where the first Orange Walks had taken place in Glasgow. So the statue, like the Walks, was part of the proud heritage of their city.

The bus swung round the Tollbooth Steeple. They'd hanged people there in the olden days. Public executions, which seemed utterly gross to Graham, but his dad had once joked with him saying that people had to have entertainment in the days when there wasn't any football.

Graham could see some boys setting up for a game of football now, on Glasgow Green, as the bus left the city centre and went down the Saltmarket past the High Court towards the Clyde. Along the riverbank the faceted dome of the mosque claimed its own place on the skyline. You got a different outlook from the top deck of a bus, Graham thought, and suddenly realized that he hardly ever travelled on a bus. He walked to school in the morning, and most times if he went anywhere, one of his parents drove him. It had been a huge tussle for him to get them to allow him to attend the Glasgow City training sessions as it meant him being out by himself later in the evenings. The river slid gunmetal-grey underneath them as they crossed the Albert Bridge and headed into the south side of the city.

Fifteen minutes later the two boys stood outside a

large house surrounded by a well-kept garden.

'This is it,' said Joe. 'It's your call. What d'you want to do?'

'Her parents don't know about Kyoul,' said Graham. 'And I'm not to let them know. Supposing one of them answers the door?'

Joe thought for a minute. 'I've got an idea,' he said. 'Hang on here. I'll go to that paper shop we passed on the main road.'

Five minutes later he returned carrying a selection of papers: the *Daily Record*, the *Evening Times*, the *Herald* and the *Scotsman*. 'If her mum or dad comes to the door we'll say we're paper boys,' Joe explained, 'and pretend we've got the wrong address.'

'And if that happens,' said Graham, 'then what?'

'We think of plan B.' Joe grinned. 'But let's hope it's Leanne who answers.'

Chapter 12

The bell chime was still sounding when a young teenage girl dressed in jeans and a short T-shirt opened the door.

'Are you Leanne?' Joe asked.

The girl hesitated. 'Who are you?'

'I'm Graham,' said Graham, 'and this is Joe. We've got a message for someone at this address. Are you Leanne?'

When she nodded Graham fumbled in his pocket and brought out Kyoul's piece of paper. 'A friend of yours asked me to bring you a message,' he said in a low voice.

Joe took a quick look behind Leanne into the hallway of the house. 'It seems clear,' he hissed at Graham.

'Kyoul.' Graham mouthed the name at Leanne.

'What?' Leanne gave them both a startled glance.

'Kyoul,' Graham repeated a shade louder.

'Kyoul?' The girl now looked scared. Her eyes opened wide. Huge dark eyes in her pretty oval-shaped face. 'What do you know about Kyoul?'

Graham handed Leanne the piece of paper Kyoul had written on. Leanne took it. She read it twice, then opened the door wider and brought them both inside the house.

'Something's happened to him,' she said, and her voice began to shake. 'Hasn't it? Something bad. What?'

Graham glanced around nervously. 'Kyoul told me to be sure your parents didn't hear,' he whispered.

'They're out visiting my gran,' said Leanne. 'They won't be back till this afternoon. Where is Kyoul?'

Graham found he couldn't say the sentence to tell Leanne that her boyfriend had been stabbed in the street. The memory of last night came rushing into his mind and his mouth wouldn't form the words. Instead of speaking he gave Leanne the mobile phone Kyoul had asked him to return.

Leanne stared into Graham's face. Then she took the phone from him and looked again at the paper in her hand. 'These marks,' she said, 'are they blood? His blood?' Her fingers trembled. 'What has happened to him? What has happened to Kyoul?'

'He's OK,' said Graham. 'I think.' The words rushed out of him. 'He got jumped by a gang in the city centre last night. They knifed him. I was passing and called the ambulance on his mobile phone and went with him to the hospital.'

'What!' cried Leanne. 'He's been stabbed! Who did it? Is he all right?'

'I think he'll be OK,' said Graham. 'When the ambulance got to the hospital they took him straight into theatre.' He looked to Joe for support. 'I mean, he should be OK. His eyes were open when I left him and – and the doctors were right there.'

'No!' Leanne clutched the piece of paper. 'No! How could this have happened? He's usually so careful.'

'It was a deserted street,' said Graham. 'I think he was taking a short cut. Like me,' he added.

'He's in hospital? Which hospital?'

She had stepped closer to Graham. He could see tears filling her eyes. 'The City Hospital. They were taking him to theatre when I left.'

'Why didn't you wait to find out how he was?' she said in a piteous voice.

'I couldn't,' said Graham. He felt guilty now. 'I'd to get home before my parents started worrying. Anyway, Kyoul said he'd tell the doctors nothing, not even his name, so I couldn't hang about in case they started asking me questions. And I had to leave because he wanted me to tell you what had happened to him. But I don't know if he's survived.'

Leanne gave a small moan, and ran her fingers through her hair. Her tears overflowed and began to run down her face. 'You said it was a knife wound. Supposing they couldn't save him? Supposing he – he's . . .' Her voice broke on a sob. 'Supposing he's died?'

Graham looked at her miserably.

'Can't you phone the hospital?' Joe suggested to Leanne.

'Oh, yes,' said Graham eagerly. 'I'd like to know how he is too.'

Leanne shook her head. 'I can't do that,' she said. 'They'd want to know who I am.' She brushed her face with her hands and managed to smile at the boys. 'Come and have a drink while I think what to do.'

She led them through the house and into a huge kitchen where her jacket and bag lay on a chair. She had been ready to go out, Graham thought. Maybe waiting for Kyoul to call her. Joe and Graham sat down while Leanne took some cans of juice from the fridge and put them on the table.

Then she sat down beside them. 'I thought there was something wrong when Kyoul didn't meet me last night and the mobile didn't answer when I called him.' She studied Graham for a minute before saying, 'That was a kind thing to do. Call the ambulance and wait with him.'

Graham's face went red but he didn't say anything.

'Did either of you tell your parents any of this?'

'No way!' said Joe at once.

'Absolutely not,' said Graham. 'I would never be allowed out on my own again.'

'I'm sorry if it's caused you a lot of bother,' said Leanne. She stood up and opened her bag. 'You really deserve a reward for coming all the way across the city.' She took out her purse. 'I'm sorry. I've only got twenty-five pounds on me at the moment. I'll give you the rest later.'

'It doesn't matter,' said Graham awkwardly.

'You must take it,' said Leanne. 'You'd to pay the bus fare to get here. And anyway,' she went on as he still hesitated, 'I'd like you to do something else for me.'

Chapter 13

'All I want you to do is find out how he is.'

Joe stood slightly to one side and watched Leanne plead with Graham.

'*Please.*' Leanne's voice began to wobble again. 'You could do this for me.'

'I don't want to go back into that hospital,' said Graham. 'They were swarming all over us last night in Accident and Emergency. They probably think that I'm one of the gang because I ran away. If they see me again they'll call the police.'

'Kyoul will have been moved from Accident and Emergency,' Leanne reasoned. 'He'll be in a ward somewhere. It won't be the same staff. You could go in at visiting time. See that he's all right. Tell him I'll try to sort something out.'

Graham shook his head. 'What do you mean "sort something out"? Sort what? There's something funny here. You're not telling us everything. Is Kyoul on drugs?'

'No way!' Leanne exclaimed. 'I swear we're not into drugs.'

'I don't really want to get involved,' said Graham.

'You're not getting involved. Just speak to Kyoul in the hospital and give him my message.' She included Joe in her tearful look this time. '*Please.*'

The boys exchanged glances.

'Then we can meet again so that you can let me know how he is,' Leanne went on. 'And I'll give you the rest of your money.'

'Never mind that,' said Graham. 'Can't we just phone you to tell you how he is?'

'Please, no. My parents might pick up the phone.'

'You could use your mobile.' Graham pointed to the phone he'd given her when they'd entered the house.

Leanne shook her head. 'I've thought about that. There will be a record of the call you made for the ambulance last night. Just in case anyone follows that up, I'm going to throw it away and say I lost it yesterday afternoon.'

Graham hesitated. 'I guess I do want to know myself that he's OK.'

'Then why don't you go and find out?' said Joe. 'Tomorrow's Sunday. Afternoon visiting will be very busy. Nobody'll notice you in the crowds. But if you think you might be recognized you could wear a baseball cap so your face won't show on the CCTV cameras.'

CCTV cameras! Graham's stomach flipped. There must have been some at the hospital last night. 'I'd forgotten the CCTV cameras.' He turned to Joe in panic. 'I'll be on the CCTV at the City Hospital. The police will know who I am.'

Joe laughed. 'The polis have got better things to do than chasing the likes of you.' He looked at Leanne. 'Kyoul's not done anything wrong, has he?'

'No-o,' she said slowly.

'What?' Graham said sharply. 'What's he done?'

'You'd better tell us,' said Joe. 'Or we're not going to help you.'

Leanne gripped her hands together in anxiety. She paced over to the window, then turned to face the two boys. 'I suppose I need to tell you if you're going to help me. But you mustn't tell anyone else.'

Graham and Joe nodded.

'Promise?'

'Aye,' the boys said together.

'He's from the Balkans. And he was smuggled into Britain by a friend. He had to get out of his own country. He was a target for a militant anti-Muslim group.' She shuddered. 'You've no idea of the things they do to people.'

'How did you meet him?' asked Graham.

'I was at one of Glasgow University's school open days. He came in off the street. He'd always hoped to go to university. We were both looking at the same stand and we got talking about what course we might take. I liked him straight away. He's really clever. And he's funny and kind.'

'Why can't he become like an ordinary asylum seeker?' said Joe. 'And get help the usual way?'

'It's complicated,' said Leanne. 'I don't know if I understand it myself exactly, but because his country is on this thing called the White List, Britain won't help him. They say these countries are safe because their governments have officially agreed they won't persecute minorities. So even if it's known that you might be killed or tortured if you went back, you still can't apply for asylum. That means no benefit. People like Kyoul are treated as though they don't exist.'

'If he was picked up by the police,' said Graham, 'what would happen to him?'

'I don't know,' said Leanne, 'and neither does he exactly. He's terrified of anybody in authority. He's only been here a few weeks. The people who brought him in left him by the side of the motorway. He lives rough most of the time.'

'Would he get deported?' asked Joe.

'He might be put in one of the detention centres.' Leanne rubbed her eyes with the back of her hand. 'I'd probably never see him again.'

'That's why he told me he wouldn't speak once the ambulance arrived!' said Graham.

'Please,' said Leanne. 'You're the only ones who can help me. I can't go myself. I don't want my parents to find out about us.' She began to cry again and pulled out another tissue to wipe her eyes. 'They just wouldn't understand.'

Joe glanced at Graham. Graham looked away.

'I can't do this,' Graham said finally.

'Of course you can,' said Joe. He moved nearer to Graham and said quietly, 'It'll be dead easy. And once you've done it you can meet Leanne and collect the rest of your reward.'

'It's dangerous,' said Graham.

Joe laughed. '*Dangerous?*'

'Well, it was dangerous for me this morning,' said Graham with feeling.

'It was only dangerous for you because you were reading your map upside down and wandered into the Promised Land.'

'The Promised Land?'

'Aye, that's what we call our bit of the city. The Promised Land.'

'You're kidding!' said Graham.

'Naw, I'm no,' said Joe.

Graham didn't answer.

Joe spoke fiercely. 'It's better than that place your granda lives.'

'What's wrong with Bridgebar?' Graham demanded.

'What's right with it?' Joe asked sarcastically.

Graham took a step towards him. 'My granda lives there. That's what's right with it.'

'Well the Garngath is a great place. Only at one time my granny says the Council used it to dump trouble-makers.'

'Exactly.'

'What are you trying to say?'

'I'm not saying anything.'

'Well, keep it that way.'

'Why are you arguing?' Leanne looked from one to the other. 'I thought you were friends.'

'We're just thinking out what to do,' said Graham tightly.

'Yeh, that's right,' Joe mumbled.

'Will you do it for me?' Leanne asked. She was crying openly now. 'Go and see if he is all right. Tell him I know where he is. That's all I'm asking.'

Graham looked at Joe helplessly. How could he refuse?

'I'll come with you,' Joe offered. Then, as Graham continued to hesitate, he added, 'I've just remembered anyway. I know someone that works in the City Hospital. I'll arrange to meet her there tomorrow and then we can ask her about Kyoul.'

'Don't tell me,' said Graham. 'It's another one of your cousins.'

Chapter 14

After the boys left Leanne sat for a while in the kitchen.

It was her favourite room in the house. Her early childhood memories had been forged here, with the smell of cooking and the sound of conversation. It had been the domain of her gran, her father's mother, who had lived with them for many years until illness meant she had to go into a nursing home.

All through her life it was this kitchen that Leanne came home to after school each day. When she was younger her grandmother would take her onto her lap, feed her scones warm from the oven and listen to all her tales of triumph and woe.

But now her beloved gran hardly knew her any more. Her mind was loosening as she got older, her thoughts drifting, touching reality less and less. Leanne's parents spent most Saturdays at the nursing home. Sometimes her gran recognized them; often she spoke to Leanne's father as though he were her husband, who'd been dead for more than thirty years. 'Where have you been, David?' she would scold him. 'I wait so long for you to come and see me. Why aren't you here when I wake up in the morning?'

Leanne's father would hold his mother's hand. 'I'm here now,' he would whisper. 'I'm here now,' and tears glistened in his eyes.

Leanne felt tears gather in her own eyes as emotions tumbled within her. She was concerned for Kyoul, but she also felt guilty. She'd told her parents she would study today, when in reality she intended to go out and meet Kyoul. She couldn't help herself, he was so kind and gentle. And, although a few years older than her, in some ways more vulnerable.

The city might have overwhelmed him if he had not met her so soon after his arrival. She'd taken him about, partly to get him orientated but also to show off her city – the shops, the cafés, the riverside, the grand buildings, the museums and galleries. He was someone who shared her interests. He'd point out things that she hadn't noticed about Glasgow. The colour of the skies, the shape of clouds, the light – he made her appreciate the spring sunsets that each evening turned the skyline into an unfolding drama.

She'd looked out for him, taught him so many things. How to ask for what he wanted when shopping. How to count money so that he didn't get cheated in his change. How to use the transport system. One Saturday they'd whizzed round and round for hours on the crazy little trains in the underground, doing the circle over and over until he knew all the subway stations. The way he said their names, his tongue layering the syllables with different emphasis, made it sound like a poem. He'd been fascinated that you could stay on as long as you wanted, endlessly travelling round under the city. Eventually, when she'd insisted they leave, he got to his feet, stood in front of her, swaying as the carriages moved, and recited all the station names without pausing.

'Cess-nock, St E-noch,
St George's Cross!
Par-tick, Kin-ning Park,
Shields Road!
Kelvin-hall, Kelvin-bridge,
Bu-chan-an Street!
Hill-head, Cow-cadd-ens,
Ibrox!
West Street, Bridge Street,
Govan!'

Kyoul finished with a great flourish of his arms and bowed low before her.

'The end!'

An old man sitting opposite solemnly applauded, and the two of them collapsed together, giggling.

Kyoul was quick to learn and fun to be with, and every morning she got up Leanne was happy with the joy of living. It was a month before he told her he was an unregistered asylum seeker. He refused to use the word 'illegal', said that there was no such thing. Britain had signed an agreement to help refugees, which meant that anyone had a right to seek safety here. He told her what country he came from. She knew then, without him having to say it, that he was a Muslim. Far from being angry with him, as he'd expected, she was frantic with worry. How did he live? What did he eat? Where did he go at night?

He found casual work, usually in the early morning at one of the big markets. He slept in homeless shelters or hostels. But he'd no friends. Friends had let him down in the past. But he trusted her. They met sometimes for only half an hour in the early evening. She'd invent a reason that her parents would believe for her being out on her own or late home from school. They thought she did an awful lot of studying in the Mitchell Library. She couldn't bring herself to tell them any part of the truth.

For she knew that he would not fit in with her parents' future hopes for her. They'd had to work hard to achieve the wealth they now enjoyed. They expected her to benefit from their sacrifice. The presence of their expectations was in the room with her now. University, good career, marriage, children – she could choose, but . . . her choice was to achieve all that she was capable of. Make the most of herself, enjoy achievement in her life. They wanted the best for her. They loved her.

With her gran so ill she felt there was no one to confide in. She'd never had one special friend to ask what to do. Kyoul was her special friend now. She talked to him of her gran.

'My grandmother was engaged at sixteen.' She was teasing him one day when she'd said this.

'But you are not yet sixteen,' he chided her.

'In your culture, don't women marry even younger?'

He looked at her, his eyes travelling over her face, her body, until she'd blushed. He'd smiled. Cupped her face in his hands. 'Little Leanne.' He stroked her cheek.

At that time they hadn't even kissed.

She loved taking him into the city. They trawled through the St Enoch shopping mall, down Sauchiehall Street into the Buchanan Galleries, through the markets and the expensive boutiques in Princes Square. One day they bought ice-cream cones and ate them wandering in the Botanic Gardens. It was the beginning of May. The warm spring sunshine had brought the residents of the nearby flats out to stroll, sit on the benches, or lie on the grass. Couples chatted, families played games, babies toddled, old people snoozed in the heat. He took her hand as they walked along. It was the most natural thing to do. They'd turned to each other. And kissed. Like that.

Now his whole life and future was in jeopardy.

In the kitchen Leanne laid her head on the table and wept.

He wouldn't take money from her. He'd found ways to live. The handouts for the homeless, the building sites where he could pick up some work. He could afford enough for the hostels, and he said as summer was coming, he would sleep outside more. So for six weeks they'd lived in this bubble and now it had blurred and was gone. One moment of violence and her happiness had disappeared. When she'd been with him she hadn't thought of the future long term; it was enough that they were together. Though Kyoul was more watchful. He'd seen the ugly side of humanity close up – had told her briefly of his imprisonment, some of the things he'd endured. So now she would have to be strong and think for him. He needed her. She must work out the best thing to do.

She had to believe that he was alive and going to survive. The boy Graham said that the doctors had attended to him as soon as the ambulance arrived at the emergency department. She herself couldn't go near the hospital. If she did she might be questioned. Then it wouldn't take them long to work out that he was an unregistered asylum seeker. It was better to keep it the way it was as long as possible, with him telling them nothing. But surely, there must be some way she could help him.

Leanne took a paper hanky from her bag. She wiped her eyes and blew her nose. Then she got up from the table and put on her jacket. She would go into the city today. But not to shop. She had some things she needed to find out.

Chapter 15

'Come away in. Come away in.'

Graham's granda was always pleased to see him. And Graham always felt safe and happy in his Granda Reid's home. He'd visited his grandparents' house in Bridgebar most every Saturday for as long as he could remember. And when his granny had died he'd kept coming each weekend as he got older. During the football season, Saturday wouldn't be Saturday without him and his granda being together. Graham hung up his jacket and followed his granda through to the living room.

'See what I've laid out for you.' From tissue paper lying on the sideboard his granda held up an orange sash edged in purple and fringed with silver. It was a very old sash of the Orange Order. Worn by his granda and his father before him. The old man began to sing softly.

'It is old but it is beautiful and its colours they are fine,
It was worn at Derry, Aughrim, Enniskillen and the Boyne.
My father wore it as a youth in bygone days of yore,
And on the Twelfth I love to wear the sash my father wore.

‘It’s the local Walk next week, Graham.’

‘Yes,’ said Graham.

‘It’s on Saturday morning. We can take part together because the Rangers game is not till the Sunday afternoon.’

‘I know, Granda.’

‘Big day for the Lodge. Makes us old yins proud to see the young yins marching. Gives us hope for the future.’

‘You told me that, Granda.’

‘Even more important nowadays as we’re under threat of restrictions.’

Graham nodded.

From under thick white eyebrows Graham’s granda looked at him with eyes that shone with love. Graham smiled back at his granda. He knew that his granda would do anything for him. And Graham didn’t want to let his granda down. The old man would be so disappointed if Graham said he wasn’t prepared to wear the sash and march this year. It didn’t seem so much to agree to: to take part in the Walk next week. But . . . he still hadn’t said yes. His parents hadn’t allowed Graham to enrol in the Juniors, even though his Granda Reid was never done telling Graham’s dad that it was a family tradition. His mum and dad had discussed it with Graham. Although his mum had sometimes taken part in the Walks when she was young, both his parents felt that he should wait until he got older. Then he could make up his own mind if he wanted to join in. This was the year Graham would decide.

‘I’m no forcing you, mind. It’s your decision.’

That’s what Graham’s dad had said. ‘It’s your decision,

Graham. You mustn't always do things to please other people, even if you love them. The big decisions in life have to be made for yourself, by yourself. Take your time. Think it over.'

Graham knew that some people didn't like the Orange Walks. Usually his mum and dad took him away on holiday at the beginning of July. But he'd seen his granda walk a few times and he could see why people objected to it. Hangers-on turned up and shouted things, mainly anti-Celtic stuff. And despite the Walk having marshals, the swearing and taunting calls persisted. 'Ignoramuses', his granda called them. 'No idea of the proper historical origins of this important tradition. We don't need eedjits to make our point for us. We walk the highway proudly as we're entitled.'

Graham's granda laid the sash carefully in the box on the sideboard and closed the lid. 'You'll come to it in your own time,' he said confidently.

Graham smiled but didn't look directly at his granda.

'We'll assemble at the Lodge next Saturday morning and walk through the city to Bridgebar Park,' his granda said, as he went through to his tiny kitchen and put some sliced sausage and black pudding under the grill. He was making plans for next weekend. 'All my pals will come to see you. Ach, there's nothing like the sound of a flute band. And when you watch them coming up the middle of the road, the noise and the colour, and the banners with their gold tassels and ribbons streaming – it's magnificent! All the wee juniors done up in their best, with their wee sashes on. Lovely. The lassies look grand and the boys so smart, all of them loyal and true.' Granda

Reid began to hum, *We'll guard old Derry's Walls*, as he made the lunch.

Graham helped him put out some plates and began to butter the bread. For the big Walk in Glasgow at the beginning of July his granda's relatives and friends came over from Ulster. 'The gathering of the clans', his granda called it. For the twelfth of July his granda was one of around fifteen thousand Scots who went over to Northern Ireland to show solidarity with their brothers and sisters across the water. It was all because from way back the Irish wouldn't stop rebelling against the Crown. Scottish soldiers were sent over to help put down the rebellions. They'd served with the Orange Yeomanry and brought back the Orange Lodge idea when they returned to Scotland. That's how it had all started. Over the years lots of Ulster Protestants had migrated to Scotland, so now the Orangemen were the oldest and biggest Protestant Fraternity in Scotland.

'True loyal origins, the Orange Order,' Granda Reid would say. 'A sash is the badge of the honest man. That's what I am. An honest Protestant man, and I'm not afraid to show it. We have to guard against False Doctrine. We march humbly but with dignity. It's a declaration of loyalty and Protestantism. Those who truly hold with the Bible will recognize the legitimacy of our ways. We testify for the truth. And that's what it's all about. The truth.

'And we've the truth of our history to protect as well. We had hard times to defend ourselves in Ulster and here in Scotland. They don't tell you that, do they? Naw. It's *their* stories you hear. *Their* Famine. Nobody mentions the atrocities *we* suffered, how the Catholics murdered men, women and children in Portadown on the banks of the Bann. And today, we've still to defend ourselves. They're trying to crush our spirit, but we will not be crushed. We will parade. But there's no offence intended to anyone, you know.'

Yet Graham's dad and his mum, who was Granda Reid's daughter, wouldn't let Graham take part in the Walks when he was growing up. They'd insisted that he wait until this year and make his own decision.

This year.

Now.

By next week Graham had to decide whether he would walk or not.

Graham smothered his sliced sausage with brown sauce and sat down to eat. The table was at the living-room window and today, because it was the Rangers–Celtic derby, his granda had put up bright-blue curtains and hung out his Ulster and Union flags and bunting, as had most of his neighbours.

'You've got to keep your end up,' his granda said as he saw Graham looking at the flag. 'Their places will be covered in green.'

Graham wasn't going to tell his granda that he knew this was true, that he had seen it this morning with his own eyes. The Garngath. Covered in green and white with the Irish flag prominent. You would have thought it was another country, not another part of the same city.

Chapter 16

While they ate lunch Granda Reid played one of his old football films and gave Graham a running commentary. He often did this before a big match. And, although Graham had seen many of them before, he never tired of watching great football play of the past. With his granda he relived Archie Gemmill's magic goal in the World Cup Finals in Argentina, when he'd beaten four men with his amazing slalom down the park. It was Gemmill, a Scottish player, who won the goal of that tournament as millions around the world applauded a golden moment of pure genius. But mostly Graham and his granda watched the Rangers team games over and over.

One summer holiday his granda had taken him all the way up to Fife to visit Jim Baxter's memorial. A special outing to pay tribute to a special footballer. 'Intelligent player,' his granda said; 'gifted . . . and cheeky.' He laughed. 'Right cheeky, he was. We've had some great players at Ibrox over the years.'

Graham loved Ibrox Park, the Rangers football ground. He'd done the tour many times. Seen the trophy room, the marble staircase and the elegant wood panelling that had come from the old *Queen Mary*, the liner that was built in the Clydebank shipyards down the river from the park itself. When Rangers played at home, being in the crowd fired him up, all singing together; he enjoyed that sense of belonging. He liked the way the stadium was constructed, sweeping round with the overlapping end, which meant that from his seat he could see the cranes along the Clyde. It was one of the landmarks he looked for when flying home from his holidays every summer.

Graham told his granda about last night's football, describing how he'd scored the winning goal.

'Sounds a bit like what Laudrup did at Tannadice when Rangers won the League Championship in nineteen ninety-seven,' said Granda Reid. 'Laudrup came steaming up the park and crashed the ball right past the goalie into the back of the net. That one's a legend. Gave us nine in a row. What a night! We all waited up till two in the morning for the team coming home to Ibrox Park.'

'Glorious goal,' agreed Graham, who had seen the video of the celebrations.

'Came off a cross by Charlie Miller.'

Graham realized, too late, the question his granda was bound to ask.

'Who supplied you?' asked the old man. 'Who set it up for you to score?'

'A team-mate.' Graham couldn't think of any way to avoid the inevitable.

'What's his name?'

'Joe,' said Graham.

'His second name?'

'Flaherty,' said Graham reluctantly.

'He'll be a Roman then?'

Graham shrugged. 'Dunno,' he said.

'You can bet your boots on it.' His granda spoke bitterly. 'They're everywhere. You can tell by their names if nothing else. Reilly, O'Connell, Doyle. They're not *Scottish* names, are they? Incomers. That's what they are. And see what they've done? Corrupted us with their false doctrine. Intermarried and polluted the race. And you'll notice in a mixed marriage the pressure's always on us to turn.'

Turn.

Turn. It made Graham think of sour milk. When his granny was alive she would tease him if he was in a bad mood by saying, 'You'll turn milk with that look.'

But that wasn't how it was used in Glasgow by older people.

He'd learned in school that the expression came from an ancient war. It was to do with uniforms and someone turning their coat to show different colours so they could fight on the other side. A turn coat. When Graham's class had been learning metaphors and similes he'd asked the teacher, 'What does "to turn" mean?' There had been a silence and some sniggering. Mr Mackintosh coughed awkwardly and said it was like during the war when someone changed allegiance. But Graham found out later what the rest of the class knew. It was to do with whether you changed from being Protestant to Catholic, whether you changed from being Kirk to going to the Chapel.

Before leaving the house Graham helped his granda

set up the television to record the game. It meant that they could watch the re-run and discuss the play afterwards. If things went fairly today Rangers should win. You couldn't guarantee it though. A biased ref (and there were plenty who favoured the other side) could mean that, despite better play, the match could swing away from them.

'We'll get started now, son, and meet up with Big Tam and Sidney and Sadie and the rest.' His granda handed Graham his jacket and they went out into the street to walk to the game.

And this was when the good feeling began. Setting out through the streets of Bridgebar to meet up with their pals. Every week, walking with them, feeling proud, Granda Reid's hand on his shoulder. Going to the game, all together, supporting *their* team. The mighty Glasgow Rangers.

Chapter 17

As they made their way along the Gallowgate towards Celtic's football ground at Parkhead Joe could feel his dad's mood begin to swing up.

Joe knew that partly it was being outside that did it. All week, when Joe was at school, his dad hardly left the house. He would never go into the city centre on his own. Even walking to the nearby shop was sometimes too much of an effort. So Saturday was special for him. A day out to support their football team, the Glasgow Celtic.

Joe saw the strain ease from his father. Like some substance leaking away from him, an insubstantial shadow withdrawing from his body. His dad turned and smiled at him. It was *almost* a grin, Joe decided. That was the strange thing about his dad's condition. Other times he could smile when people were around, pretend he was OK in company. Especially when Joe's granny, who was his own ma, was there. It grieved her to see her son in this condition and Joe's dad was good at making a quip or two to keep her from asking how he was.

His dad tilted his face to the sky, and closed his eyes

as the sun warmed him. Joe noticed how pale and wasted he appeared. He must try to get him out in the evenings during the week, now that the summer was nearly here.

'Routine,' the doctor had told Joe. 'Routine is good. Set up a structure to his life. But he does need a lot of support in doing that.'

They turned down Janefield Street. And now they were with their own. The streets vibrant with green and white. Team colours, scarves, new strips, memorial tops, many wearing the magical Number Seven, some showing the face of Celtic's former striker, Henrik Larsson. Outside one of the pubs they met up with Joe's Aunt Rita's brother, Desmond, and one or two of his mates. Joe knew that his dad thought Desmond was a bit of a screwball but he was good fun to be with, full of wild stories and tales of his exploits when following the team to their away games all over Europe.

'Aw right, wee man?' Desmond slung his arm round Joe's shoulder and grabbed him.

'Less of the wee man,' laughed Joe, pushing Desmond away.

'Oh. Oh.' Desmond retreated in mock fright. 'How's the football training? Score any goals lately?'

'Naw, but I set one up for our centre mid-field player last night, so I think I might be in with a chance of getting picked for the team.'

'What mid-field player? Anyone I know?'

'Don't think so,' said Joe, sensing what was coming next.

'Does he no go to your school then?'

'Naw.'

'Don't tell me he's a Hun?'

'His name's Gregory,' said Joe. 'Does that sound like a Hun to you?'

'You can never tell nowadays. What with Catholics being called after stars instead of saints.'

'He's a terrific football player,' said Joe. 'Him and me work great together, but we need more practice.'

'Come to Glasgow Green tomorrow and me and the boys'll play kick-about with you.'

'I'll see,' said Joe. 'I might phone you later. I've got something I need to do in the afternoon.'

They were at the ground now, and to get to their entrance they had to walk round the lines of mounted police. The horses stood patiently, their heads protected by clear face-guards, as the police shouted instructions and herded the fans into the correct queue for the turnstiles. Over at the London Road end Joe could see the Rangers fans being channelled to their section of the ground, kept apart by temporary steel barricades and squads of security guards and policeman.

Among the Rangers fans Granda Reid's friend Sidney had stopped to chat to one of the street vendors who was selling flags and scarves. Graham could hear him hooting with laughter at some joke.

Graham looked over to the front of the Celtic Parkhead stadium. Thousands of fans swarmed outside, meeting up and calling to friends.

'I'm keeping these hidden the now,' Sidney said as he caught up with them. He opened his hand. In his palm were a couple of potatoes. 'The polis are so paranoiac at Old Firm games, if they see these I'd get arrested for carrying a dangerous weapon.' He grinned at Graham as he shoved the potatoes in his pocket. 'They'll be good for a wind-up later on.'

Chapter 18

Graham and his Granda Reid got to their seats.

When the match was at Parkhead, the Celtic ground, the Rangers fans were allocated a corner of the Lisbon Lions Stand. Double lines of stewards with empty seats in between separated the two groups of supporters. Graham didn't always get a ticket when the match was held at Parkhead Stadium. It was strange, and off-putting, having to face into tier upon tier of green and white. He wondered where Joe and his dad sat to watch the game.

Granda Reid and Graham stood up to sing *Simply the Best* as the Rangers team came out of the tunnel. They *were* better than all the rest. Second to none. Part of the beating heart of this great city.

Joe was on his feet as the Celtic players ran onto the pitch. His voice combined with all the other fans roaring out their welcome to the people's team. The city itself threw back the sound and folded him in.

The game began.

There was always more tension at an Old Firm game

than at any other. A tang of bitterness. Graham thought that it sometimes took away the enjoyment of the actual football, but he would never say this to his granda. He knew that in his granda's opinion the only thing that counted in an Old Firm game was the result. And this was an important game. It was almost the last game of the League Championship. Both teams sat at the top of the league table, closely followed by Hearts. With no goal difference between any of them, it could be a decider. They needed Rangers to go ahead today.

They didn't have long to wait.

In the nineteenth minute, Houston, Rangers' new star striker, charged through, unleashed a stinging right kick, and lashed the ball home.

Houston had scored! With the rest of the Rangers fans Graham catapulted to his feet. They had a goal! Despite being away from home and in the minority, all around him Rangers shouts and songs began to drown out the Celtic supporters' boos and whistles.

Now they were bouncing. Jumping up and down. And yelling themselves hoarse. Rangers were ahead! And in only nineteen minutes too! It was going to be a fabulous day.

'Hello! Hello!
We are the Billy Boys!
Hello! Hello!
You'll know us by our noise!'

Graham danced around. Stamping and clapping. His granda was ecstatic.

'Quality shows.' His granda beamed at him. 'Quality shows.'

In response to the crowd Rangers lifted their performance even higher, and for the rest of the first half Celtic were left chasing the game.

Just before half time the Rangers support rose and sang a salute to their team to carry them through the break.

'There's not a team like the Glasgow Rangers.
No, not one! No, not one!
Celtic know all about their troubles,
We will fight till the day is done.
There's not a team like the Glasgow Rangers,
No, not one! No, not one!'

What must it feel like to be on the park? Graham wondered. Hearing the support. Surfing that sound.

'They'll be demoralized for the second half,' said Granda Reid as they trooped out of their seats. 'We're one up. They're down. Let's hope it stays like that. Us on top. The way we should be.'

'Aye, and they don't have Larsson to sort their problems out for them now,' gloated Sidney.

Further over in the Lisbon Lions Stand Desmond had his head in his hands.

'Where's Henrik Larsson when we need him?' he moaned.

'Life without Larsson,' said Joe's dad. 'Good title for a poem, that.'

'You write one then,' said Desmond aggressively.

'It would be a lament,' said Joe's dad. 'A dirge. *De Profoundis we cry to thee, Henrik. Come back to your kingdom, O King of Kings.*'

'Joseph, you annoy me stupit the way you don't take anything seriously,' said Desmond.

'*Au contraire*,' said Joe's dad. 'My doctor tells me that I take things far too seriously.'

'I'm talking here about things that *matter*,' Desmond retorted. 'Really important things.'

Joe interrupted as his dad opened his mouth to reply. 'Let's get something to eat,' he said. 'I'm starving.'

Queuing for Bovril and hot snacks, they watched the replay over and over on the TV screens set above the bar. The comments were non-stop.

'Flaming ridiculous, that goal, so it was.'

'Shouldn't have been allowed, that.'

'He was offside.'

'Aye, *well* offside.'

'Dirty Hun.'

'Mah-*nure*!'

'That ref's a bigoted b—'

Returning to their seats after half time, they passed the doors to one of the bar areas which was locked today as it was in the Rangers supporters' section of the ground.

'See that?' Joe's Uncle Desmond pointed to the blacked-out glass windows. 'That's so they can't see us. During Old Firm games they stick bin liners over the glass on they doors so that the Huns can't give us the finger and try to cause aggro. Animals, so they are. Animals.'

Joe remembered Graham saying this morning that his Granda Reid went early to the Old Firm games to avoid any trouble. As they were going upstairs Joe turned his head and looked back at the blacked-out door.

Graham was on the other side of that darkened glass.

Chapter 19

One down.

Losing to the enemy.

A goal gone to them.

It lay like a cold pie in the pit of Joe's belly.

Unthinkable defeat. Celtic had their last league game next Sunday against Hearts while Rangers would play Kilmarnock. If Celtic lost by any margin to Rangers this week, then Rangers would almost certainly win the Championship.

The play went on.

Ten minutes to the end of the match.

They began to sing. Quietly at first.

A few brave voices, from the terraces high above where Joe sat. He turned to his dad and grinned as they both heard the familiar opening lines of *You'll Never Walk Alone*.

'If that doesn't lift them, nothing will.'

The singers had started slowly, pacing the first words, allowing the song to unfurl. Pulling like a powerful undercurrent.

'You have to sing along with that one, Dad,' said Joe.

His dad nodded. 'It's a song of such tremendous human spirit,' he said, 'yet it always makes me want to cry.'

Rippling from row to row, the pulsing, throbbing tune was carried by the throat of each fan. The crowd caught the mood and it became unstoppable.

The great rolling anthem gathered strength.

Taken up by the people beside Joe, sweeping round the stadium, drowning out everything else, soaring and soaring. The singing rose to a deafening crescendo, pulling him out of his seat to join in.

A song of defiance, of courage, but above all, hope.

Every Celtic supporter on their feet.

Kerr had the ball. He was running to goal.

'Pass it! Pass it!' Joe's dad cried out. 'Carmichael's in the clear!'

Desmond was incandescent. 'Give it to Carmichael, you great big galoot!'

'To Carmichael!' Joe screamed. 'To Carmichael!'

Kerr tried his own shot. The goalie punched the ball aside. A Rangers defender gathered it and booted it down the park.

Joe, his dad, and Desmond fell back into their seats, energy spent.

'I could've done that better myself,' Desmond growled.

The Rangers end bawled their appreciation of their keeper's save:

'North, South, East or West,
Glasgow Rangers are the best.'

★ ★ ★

The game went on.

Insults and jibes were thrown back and forth among the supporters. The Rangers fans gesticulated and goaded those in the Celtic seats closest to them.

'Where's your *Fields of Athenry* now? Eh?'

'Tottie fields, mair like it!'

A shower of potatoes flung by Rangers fans in the front seats cascaded onto the park.

In an instant Desmond was on his feet. 'I'll go over there and batter their melt in!' he bellowed.

'Save your breath,' Joe's dad advised Desmond. 'Watch the play.'

'Never mind the play!' Desmond foamed. 'It's a goal we want!'

'Our team need your support,' said Joe's dad.

'You're right.' Desmond got to his feet and began his own song.

'Stand up if you hate the 'Gers,
If you hate the Teddy Bears!
All on your feet now!
Stand up if you hate the 'Gers!'

Joe's dad shook his head. He grabbed Desmond's sleeve and dragged him into his seat. 'Keep your attention on the field of play,' he said. 'Look! Carmichael's carving open their defence!'

Joe craned forward. His dad was right.

Under the desperate onslaught of Celtic the Rangers defence was buckling. Wave upon wave of Celtic players hurled themselves forward. Vaughan, and Dignam, a late substitute for Celtic, were relentless, creating chance after chance, as Sutton and Thompson had done for Larsson in the great days gone by. And Carmichael, slicing in, found a gap. Pouncing on a cut-back from Dignam, Carmichael nutmegged the Rangers' keeper.

The ball was in the back of the net.

Celtic had scored!

Four minutes to go! And Celtic had equalized!

Now they were jubilant. Many on their feet, singing,

'Sure it's a grand old team to play for,
It's a grand old team . . .'

The euphoria and relief of the Celtic fans continued:

'We don't care what the Rangers say,
What the hell do we care?
'Cos we only know
That there's going to be a show,
And the Glasgow Celtic will be there . . .'

Fast clapping, they began to shout, '*C'mon the Hoops! C'mon the Hoops!*'

Over and over, round the stadium: '*C'mon the Hoops! C'mon the Hoops!*'

As the supporters beside him took up the refrain, Joe stood up, yelling at the top of his voice, '*C'mon the Hoops! C'mon the Hoops!*'

The Rangers fans shouted a mocking echo: '*C'mon the Choobs! C'mon the Choobs!*'

★ ★ ★

Both sides were still shouting when the final whistle went.

'Aye, yous are no so smart now! Are yous?' Desmond turned and bawled at the Rangers fans. 'You shower of animals!'

'*Animals! Animals!*'

Groups of fans began pointing at the corner which held the Rangers supporters.

'*Animals! Animals!*'

Joe heard his own voice joining in. But the space immediately to his right was quiet. His dad had not stood up. He remained seated, applauding the teams leaving the field.

Joe fell silent. He took a swig from his can. Then he sat back down beside his dad.

Chapter 20

Outside the park the disappointment and frustration among the supporters rumbled on.

Graham and his Granda Reid got through the gates with their friends and moved away from the ground, walking quickly back to his granda's house.

Joe and his dad and Desmond were stalled as they came round the stadium and it took them longer to get onto the street. The crowds here were dense and the rain was coming on so they decided to cut across an open lane that connected to the Gallowgate. Desmond was kicking cans and anything else that lay in the street as his bad temper began to overflow. His agitation was infectious. When they met up with anyone he knew he bad-mouthed players from both sides, the manager and the referee.

'Give it a rest, Desmond,' said Joe's dad.

'I pay good money for my season ticket. It's not cheap. These guys are making millions at my expense. I'm entitled to my say.'

'I won't talk to you when you're like this, Desmond.' There was a finality in Joe's dad's voice.

To one side of the lane a group of youths sat on some

railings. Two or three of them were stripped to the waist, with green-and-white flags and scarves tied about their heads and shoulders. They were singing ragged snatches of songs and passing a bottle of alcohol wrapped in a plastic carrier between them.

'As if the polis are fooled by that,' Joe's dad commented as they came level with them.

Desmond broke away to speak to them. Joe saw one of them offer his uncle the bottle. Desmond took it and drank.

Joe's dad shook his head.

Joe heard Desmond tell the youths about the Rangers fans throwing potatoes onto the park near time-up.

'We never saw that,' said one of the boys.

'They wouldn't have got away with it if I'd been there,' said another.

Desmond took a potato from his pocket. 'They shouldn't get away with it now,' he said.

Joe's dad took Joe firmly by the arm and steered him to the far side. 'There's a whole load of Rangers fans standing at the top end of that lane,' he explained.

'The polis are up ahead,' said Joe.

'Not enough of them.' Joe's dad's eyes were troubled. He increased his pace, pulling Joe along with him.

Joe glanced back.

He couldn't see exactly what happened. But next minute, to howls of fury from both sides, potatoes and coins were flying through the air.

Joe's dad put him to the inside of the pavement. 'Pull your jacket over your head,' he ordered Joe. 'Tuck your face in. Quickly now.'

Joe was too interested in what was happening to fully obey his dad.

Close beside Joe a woman screamed as a coin hit her on the cheek. There was a trickle of blood on her face. A young child began wailing. Adults picked up their children and began to hurry away as, to the sound of shattering glass, men and boys in Rangers colours came running down the lane.

'Get into them!'

'Celtic scum!'

An old man stood in the middle of the street and shouted at the top of his lungs: 'Tan their hides! Tan their bluebottle hides for them!'

A boy not much older than Joe, wearing a Union flag T-shirt, ran over and kicked him on the legs.

Two mounted police at the corner of the road turned their horses towards them.

'The horses!' Joe gasped.

Joe's dad grabbed him by the shoulder and shunted him against the wall.

Joe felt his father's face close to his. His body covering him with his own. He could smell his dad's skin, the wet of the rain on his hair, the sweat of fear. His dad spread his arms to protect him as the horses galloped past and on towards the fighting men.

'Don't look back,' his dad said. He grabbed Joe's hand and pulled him on.

But Joe did. He saw the brawling group scatter as the horses thundered among them.

When they were well away from the trouble Joe and his dad stopped.

‘That Desmond,’ said Joe’s dad. ‘He’ll land up in the jail one day.’

‘Shouldn’t we try to find him?’ asked Joe.

‘No,’ his dad said emphatically. ‘The thing about Desmond is, he’d take you down with him. Let’s hope the polis chase him all the way into the Clyde and it cools him off a bit. You’ll find that your Uncle Desmond can look after himself even though he causes chaos all around him. He’ll turn up at your Aunt Kathleen’s house tomorrow, looking for his dinner and full of the chat.’

As they came onto the High Street Joe’s dad said, ‘Roll your scarf up, son, and put it in your pocket. I think we’ll get the bus up the road tonight.’

Chapter 21

On Sunday morning Graham woke early.

Unless Rangers won he never felt good after an Old Firm game. Saturday's match, ending in a one-all draw, left a slightly sour taste. Unfinished business, that's what it was. Next Sunday's league games were with Hearts and Kilmarnock. So it would be a full week before the League was decided. Then Rangers and Celtic would meet again in the Cup Final at the end of May.

Yesterday, with the final whistle gone, a light drizzle had started to fall and, very subdued, they had all headed back to his granda's house through the wet streets of Glasgow. Graham had been glad when his dad had arrived early to collect him. His granda told his friends Sidney and Sadie how he was hoping Graham would be in the Orange Walk next week. Sadie spoke to Graham in the kitchen, saying that the old man might not have many years left and how much it meant to him. 'It's about sticking together,' she said. 'Family and loyalty. These things are even more important when you get older. And you're his only grandchild, his grandson. He's looking to you to carry on the tradition so the line won't be broken. You should think about that, Graham.'

They'd all had a drink and played and replayed the contentious parts of the game on the television that clearly displayed the bias of the referee. For his own interest Graham would have liked to watch the action showing Carmichael's run-through as he'd muscled aside the defence. But he didn't dare tell his granda that he wanted to study the technique of Celtic's striker. He'd managed to get home in time to record the late-night highlights on his own TV. As soon as he got a chance he'd study the Celtic player's positioning when he'd picked up on the cross to score the goal. But this morning's problem was how to get out on his own.

At breakfast Graham told his parents that he'd arranged to meet some members from his football training sessions at lunch time to have a kick-about on Glasgow Green. No, he didn't want them to come and watch. No really, thanks all the same. It was just a boys get-together. In fact if they insisted on being there he wouldn't bother. They eventually agreed he could go, as long as Graham's dad gave him a lift into the city and met at least one of the other boys. Also Graham had to promise to phone and let them know when he was coming home.

'You'll be careful, won't you?' Graham's dad said as they came into the city centre where the streets were crowded with shoppers and street traders.

Graham nodded.

'Your mum and I have only your best interests in mind when we warn you about the dangers you might face when you're out with your friends.'

'Yes, Dad.'

'Shall I read you the list?'

Graham sighed. 'I'll do it for you if you like.'

His dad grinned. 'Go on then.'

Graham took a deep breath. '*Don't do drugs. Don't do drink. Don't nick anything, even for a laugh or a dare. A police record doesn't help later in life. Don't go with strangers. Don't pick up a syringe. Don't go with the crowd if something inside you is telling you no.*

'*Don't. Don't. Don't,*' he finished wearily.

At the far end of Glasgow Green his dad turned the car in front of the ornate façade of the old Templeton's carpet factory and stopped a short distance from the People's Palace. Graham could see Joe waiting for him at the entrance. He jumped out of the car. Graham's dad lowered the car window and beckoned.

Joe came over.

'This is Joe,' said Graham.

'Hi,' said Joe.

'I hear you're a good football player,' said Graham's dad.

Joe grinned. 'I am,' he said. He jerked his thumb at Graham. 'He's no bad either.'

Graham's dad smiled. 'OK,' he said. As he put the car into gear and made to pull away he called out the window to the two boys. '*Do* enjoy yourselves this afternoon.'

'What did you tell your parents about today?' Joe asked Graham as soon as they were alone.

Graham pointed to his rucksack. 'I brought my football gear. Said we were doing some extra training together.'

'Could do,' said Joe. 'After we've done the business at the hospital. My Uncle Desmond said yesterday he'd be around today. I could phone him if you like.'

Graham shrugged. 'We'll see how this goes.' He knew that when Joe had met up with his uncle yesterday it would probably have been at the Old Firm game, but he didn't want to refer to that.

For his part Joe didn't mention that Desmond was not actually *his* uncle, but Jammy's. As far as Joe was concerned Jammy and his relatives were harmless, but he didn't want to put the frighteners on Graham. Instead he said, 'OK. Let's get *this* game over with first. If we cross London Road and go on to the Gallowgate, we can jump on a bus that'll get us to the City Hospital in time for visiting. C'mon, we'll cut through The Barras.'

Chapter 22

Graham followed as Joe went past Glickman's sweetie shop and plunged through the busy market stalls that sold everything from second-hand tat and genuine antiques to goods you could buy in the shops – sometimes even before they were available in the shops. Football memorabilia crowded in with picture postcards and vinyl LPs. Interesting historical memorabilia side by side with utter junk.

Young guys stood on corners selling any number of items. From stalls and the backs of vans people called on customers: 'Get your DVDs here! Quick now! Snap up a bargain! See the latest movies! *Before* the stars themselves! *Before* the film premiere! *Before* the polis arrive!'

'Worth coming for the patter alone,' said Graham, smiling.

'I need a minute.' Joe stepped off the street into an ornate doorway.

'Hang on,' said Graham, as he took in the sign outside:

ST FRANCISCUS CATHOLIC CHURCH

'I'm not going in there.' He grabbed Joe's arm. 'What are you up to?'

'I've got something I have to do.'

'Like what?'

'Just *something*.' Joe shook Graham's hand free.

'I'll *just* wait out here then.'

'Are you scared to come inside?' Joe challenged him.

'No,' said Graham. He followed Joe into the interior of the building and hung back at the door as Joe went over to a stand of candles. A man who might be a priest came walking up the main aisle. Supposing this man said something to him? He wouldn't know how to answer. Weren't you supposed to call them 'Father' or something? No way could he do that. And what if the man asked him a question? He'd know straight away that Graham wasn't a Catholic. Graham went over beside Joe. 'Whatever you're doing, hurry up,' he hissed.

'OK, OK.'

'What *are* you doing anyway?'

'Putting up a candle,' said Joe.

'*What!*'

'It's for my ma,' said Joe. 'Since she died a few years ago I always do it if I pass this church. Right?' he added belligerently.

Graham glanced around. He'd seen pictures of Catholic churches, with all their decorations and ornaments, but he had never actually been inside one before. There were statues *everywhere*. 'Jeez-oh,' he muttered.

'It's a very traditional church,' Joe explained as he saw

Graham looking about him. 'My granny likes it. My ma was buried from here,' he added.

'It's manic, so it is,' said Graham.

'Manic?'

'Aye. There's too much . . . *stuff* in your churches,' said Graham.

'How d'you mean *stuff*?'

'Like *tons* of things. Crosses and candlesticks and crucifixes and altars and wee coloured lamps here and there.'

Joe looked around, not seeing it as Graham did. How could he express to Graham the solid safety of his Faith? The knowledge that, if he ever had to lean back, there would be something there to support him.

'And statues . . .' Graham flapped his hands. 'There's *hunners* of statues in here.'

'Yeh, but they're to different people,' explained Joe.

'What d'you need so many for?'

'They're the saints,' said Joe. 'You can pray to them for special intentions.'

'There is only one God.' Graham was quoting his granda. 'If you believe in anything at all, then there can be only one Creator,' he added with more conviction.

'Aye, I know,' Joe replied. 'But with us . . . religion, well it's a whole life thing. Like, what you are, and who you are. And it's good to have lots of people to help you in different ways.'

'They all look the same to me,' said Graham.

'Naw, naw,' said Joe. He pointed to a statue behind them. 'That's St Therese. You know it's her because she's got the crucifix and the roses. And she helps foreign missionaries.'

'It's just – just . . .' Graham paused. He stopped short at using the word 'superstition' while Joe was standing inside his church lighting a candle for his mother who was dead. 'It's . . . it's made-up stuff.'

'You're wrong,' said Joe. 'There's a point to it. They each have their own stories. You learn about the things they did so that the way they lived their lives can help you with yours. Even *you* must've heard of St Christopher helping travellers. He carried Jesus over a river. I mean, that's what his name means – Christopher, carrier of Christ. It's my confirmation name. That's how I know.'

'Oh aye, I've heard of him,' said Graham. He looked up. 'What's that one there? The one with the wee house. Who's she? Goldilocks?'

'None of your cheek,' said Joe. 'She's St Brigid. My granny used to pray to her because her own name is Brigid and she couldn't get a house when she came to Scotland at first. And then she got one. See? It worked.'

Not that well, thought Graham, if Joe's family had ended up in the Garngath.

'Who's that one with the sore leg and the dog?' he asked. 'What's his speciality?'

'St Roch,' said Joe. 'He, em . . . his dog, em. I don't know much about him. But this is my favourite,' he added quickly, pointing to a statue of a monk cradling a dove in his hands. 'He's St Francis and he liked animals.'

Graham followed as Joe walked round the church.

'There's St Andrew.' Joe was not to be stopped. 'The patron saint of Scotland. He's got his cross, see? That's how we got our Scottish flag.'

'I know that,' said Graham.

'St Anthony – finds things that are lost.'

'Is there one that'd help us win through the football trials?' asked Graham.

'We could try St Jude. In fact' – Joe gave Graham a wicked grin – 'you could've given him a wee try yourself yesterday. He might've been able to help your team play a bit better.'

Graham looked at Joe. 'Go on then, tell me. What's he for?'

'Hopeless cases,' said Joe.

Graham decided to punch him, church or no church.

Joe skipped out of reach, laughing. 'Fell for that one,' he said. The boys jostled with each other until shushed by a woman sitting in a pew.

Before leaving Joe stretched out his hand over the candle and let the flame touch the skin of his palm for a second. Then he drew his hand away and bunched his fingers into a fist.

'It was after my ma died that my dad got depression.' Joe volunteered the information as the boys left the church together.

Chapter 23

Before they entered the grounds of the City Hospital Graham rammed his baseball cap down on his forehead.

'This doesn't cover enough of my face,' he complained.

'What do you suggest?' Joe asked in a sarcastic tone of voice. 'A mask? That might just attract a bit more attention.'

'It's all right for you to talk smart,' said Graham. 'But I'm the one who might be recognized.'

Joe's cousin was waiting for him in the café near the front door.

'This is my cousin Bernadette,' said Joe. 'Bernie, this is Gra— Gregory. We play football together.'

Joe's cousin Bernie looked at Graham/Gregory before turning her attention to Joe. 'What kind of trouble are you in?' she demanded.

'Nothing,' said Joe breezily.

'Don't "nothing" me, Joseph Flaherty. I used to change your nappies when I babysat for your parents. The patient you asked me to find out about is in ward four hundred and two under supervised visiting. What's your interest in him?'

'Oh I remember you babysitting me, Cousin Bernadette.' Joe grinned cheekily at the young woman sitting opposite him. 'Especially when I got older, 'cos while you were supposed to be watching me so that I didn't get up to any mischief, you took the time to nick my ma's fags from the kitchen cupboard.'

Bernie grinned at him. 'You wee spy,' she said. 'Don't try to blackmail me, *Cousin* Joe. What are you up to?'

'If you must know,' Joe went on, 'Gregory and me and some of our mates that play football together are sure we've seen the guy that's in your hospital at our sports ground a couple of times. Somebody said they'd read in the paper that he'd been attacked. We think he might've got jumped taking a short cut down Reglan Street on Friday night.'

'That's where the ambulance picked him up,' said Bernie.

Joe turned to Graham. 'I knew it was him!'

Graham nodded cautiously.

'Me and Gregory always go home together out the main gate,' Joe explained carefully, 'but there's a hole in the fence at the far side of the park, and we wondered if he'd gone that way. Then someone told us they'd read it in the *Evening Times* that he was in the City Hospital so I thought you'd be the person to ask.'

'Do you know anything else about this guy?' Bernie spoke seriously. 'Is it possible that he's part of a gang?'

Joe shrugged. 'Dunno. He's nothing to do with us, by the way. Not part of our football training. Don't know his name even. Oh no, wait a minute.' He looked at Graham. 'Is it Kayel, or something?'

'Dunno.' Graham shook his head.

'*Kyoul*,' said Bernie. 'He claims he's got some kind of amnesia and can't remember anything. But one of the paramedics said that the person who came with him in the ambulance called him Kyoul. So we know his name, but that's all.'

Graham ducked his head at the mention of the ambulance.

Joe nodded easily. 'Kyoul,' he said. 'That's it. And he's got amnesia, you say?'

'Well, maybe,' said Bernie. 'At any rate he won't give them any information at all, not even his age. I spoke to one of the nurses up there. They don't know if he's telling the truth when he says that he has no memory, or if it's an act he's putting on because he's got something to hide. He was certainly in shock. If the ambulance had been any later he'd have been DOA.'

'So he's going to be all right?' Graham asked her.

'He should make a full recovery from the stabbing. But . . .'

Joe put on a serious voice. 'Don't tell us anything that might get you into trouble with your superiors. I don't want you breaking your hypocritic oath.'

'*Hippocratic* oath, numpty. Nurses don't take the Hippocratic oath.' Bernie hesitated. 'We don't know anything about him. But I'll say this, that young man has been in trouble at some time. You stay away from him.' She glanced at both boys. 'Maybe you should tell the police what you know.'

Graham's stomach heaved, but Joe just smiled. 'I don't think so, Bernie. We talk to the polis, and they come calling at my house up in the Garngath to question me on something that I know nothing about. You know how *very* polite and well-mannered some polis are when they're making enquiries up there. I'd probably get cuffed and hauled off for a night in the cells. How much would that upset my da? Eh?'

Bernie's face softened. 'I hear Uncle Joseph's getting a bit better?'

'He is,' said Joe. 'So let's keep it that way. He certainly doesn't need any grief at the moment.'

'No,' said Bernie, 'but still . . . That boy might have been killed and the police are still looking for the person who was there when the ambulance arrived. I want you to tell some adult in the family who's close to you.'

'Aw, no way,' said Joe.

'Yes,' said Bernie. 'Otherwise *I* will.'

Joe thought quickly. 'I'll speak to my Auntie Kathleen.'

'Soon?'

'We usually go to her house for dinner on a Sunday night. I'll tell her then.'

'You'd better.' Bernie stood up. 'I need to go. The hospital's been going like a fair all night after that Old Firm game yesterday.' She ruffled Joe's hair. 'I'll phone sometime next week and see how things are with you.'

When she'd gone Graham let his breath out in a big sigh. 'Well, that takes care of that. We can't have any more to do with Kyoul.'

'How no?' asked Joe.

'You heard what your cousin said. He's trouble.'

'Ocht, rubbish. We gave our word to Leanne. We owe it to her to at least try to speak to him.'

'And how are we going to do that?'

'Go and see him. Bernie told us where he is. Ward four hundred and two.'

'Sorry. I'll ask you that again,' said Graham. 'How are we going to do that *without getting caught*. Or didn't you hear her? Your cousin also told you that Kyoul was under supervision.'

'At least let's go and have a look-see.' Joe indicated the front door. 'It's getting busier as folk arrive for visiting time. We'll mingle with some families and go up to the fourth floor and have a snoop.'

Chapter 24

'We can do this. No bother.'

The boys were standing in the corridor outside ward 402, Joe trying to persuade Graham to go in. 'We'll attach ourselves to the next group of visitors,' he said. 'There's loads of folk coming and going, and nowadays the hospitals are always short-staffed.' He manoeuvred Graham through the doors.

Graham gripped Joe's arm as he sauntered down the ward.

'I'll bet it's that bed right at the far end,' he muttered nervously. 'The one with the curtains drawn around it.'

'OK,' said Joe. 'You get in behind that curtain and find out.'

'There's a notice pinned to the curtain,' said Graham from the corner of his mouth. 'I can read it from here. It says: NO VISITORS – SEE MEMBER OF STAFF.'

'You could go up to the top of the bed next to his, beyond where the sink is on the wall, and edge your way in,' suggested Joe.

'What are *you* going to do?'

'I'll keep guard for you. If anybody comes I'll start

whistling.' Joe made a face at Graham. 'I'll make it *The Sash* if you like.'

'Very funny,' said Graham. 'You won't be able to get away with standing about the ward. Someone's bound to ask what you're up to.'

'I won't just be standing about. Look, there's a man in the bed next to Kyoul. I'll give him a wee visit.'

'You can't just sit down and start talking to somebody you've never met before.'

'How no?'

'He might call a nurse.'

'It'll be OK.'

'How'll it be OK? He doesn't know you.'

'I'll just say I'm Jimmy's boy.'

'What makes you think he'll know somebody called Jimmy?'

'This is Glasgow,' said Joe. 'Who *doesn't* know somebody called Jimmy?'

'You're off your head, you are,' said Graham.

Joe gave Graham a push. 'Go on. Walk to the top of that man's bed where he can't see you. He's got his eyes closed the now. I'll be close behind you. If he wakes up I'll start talking to him. You keep your eye on the main ward. As soon as you think nobody's watching, slip behind the curtain and have a quick word with Kyoul.'

Graham walked reluctantly with Joe to the end of the ward. When they reached the bed next to the one with the drawn curtain Joe propelled Graham in front of him until he was at the top end, close to the curtain of the next bed.

Joe disentangled one of the two stacked visitors' chairs

and sat down. The man in the bed's eyes fluttered.

'Mr Sinclair?' said Joe, reading the name from the piece of card attached to the bed's headrail.

Mr Sinclair opened his eyes. 'What? What is it?'

'I'm Jimmy's boy. He heard you were in the hospital and he sent me over to see you.'

'Jimmy?' The man in the bed swivelled his eyes slowly and took in Joe. 'Jimmy?' he repeated.

'Aye . . . *Jimmy*,' said Joe with more emphasis. 'He told me you used to hang about together. Said you haven't seen each other for ages, right enough.'

'Oh, *that* Jimmy.' The puzzled expression cleared from Mr Sinclair's face. 'Oh aye, it's years since I've seen him.'

Joe nodded encouragingly. 'He's no well or he'd have come his self.'

The man struggled up in bed. 'See's my teeth, there, son, would you?'

Joe heard Graham snigger as he grubbed about on the top of the locker beside the bed looking for Mr Sinclair's false teeth. Holding the plastic container they were in at arm's length, Joe handed them over.

The old man slurped them around his mouth until he had them in a satisfactory position. 'What's up with him?'

'What?' said Joe.

'What's up with him?'

'What's up with who?'

'*Jimmy*. You said he wasn't well. What's up with him?'

'Oh right.' Joe fumbled. 'Em, he's . . . it's his back . . . you know.'

'Oh aye?'

'He can hardly move.'

Mr Sinclair shook his head sympathetically. 'Always had bother with his back, Jimmy, so he did.'

'This is the worst it's been,' said Joe. 'For a while.'

'Does he get out much at all?'

'Emm . . . Em . . .' Joe groped around. 'Just to the bowls, like.'

'The bowls!' Mr Sinclair exclaimed. 'The bowls? He used to hate the bowls. Said it was a game for big lassies.'

'Aye, well . . .' Joe flashed his eyes at Graham. Graham gave a tiny wave of his hand and moved closer to the curtain of the neighbouring bed.

'No wonder he's knackered his back then, if he's taken up bowls,' Mr Sinclair observed.

'Aye, well, he watches the games mostly now . . . on the telly, like.'

'Does he? That's a surprise to me, I'll tell you. I'd never have taken Jimmy for a bowls man.'

'No?'

'Naw. Fifteen year I knew your da. And I never once heard him say a good word about the bowls. It just shows you. You think you know someone, and then they catch you out.'

'Do you like the bowls yourself, Mr Sinclair?' asked Joe, gesticulating to Graham to get on with it.

Graham slipped behind the curtain.

'Naw. I'm more into the football.'

'You're no a Tim, are you?' said Joe.

'Do I look like a Tim?' the man asked in horror.

'Aye.' Joe laughed. 'But then folk say I do too.'

'Aye, but you *do*.'

'See what I mean?' Joe laughed again, more confidently.

Mr Sinclair joined in the laughter.

'So' – Joe settled himself in his chair – 'what did you think of that result yesterday? Eh? Were we robbed, or were we robbed?'

Chapter 25

On the other side of the curtain Graham smiled. He knew Joe could talk on the subject of football long enough for him to speak to Kyoul.

He glanced around and then crept closer to the bed.

Kyoul lay on his back. His eyes were open and he was staring at the ceiling. There was a drip with a plastic tube connected to his arm. His pyjama top was open, showing his bandaged chest. Suddenly, sensing that he was not alone, he turned his head and his gaze met Graham's. There was a look of terror on his face.

'Don't panic.' Graham held up his hand. 'It's only me. Remember? I called the ambulance for you on Friday night.'

Kyoul fixed an expressionless gaze on Graham's face.

'In the street. Reglan Street,' Graham said. 'I was the one who helped you.'

Recognition and relief flooded Kyoul's features. 'Did you find Leanne's house? Did you speak to her?' he asked at once.

Graham nodded. 'She knows what happened and where you are.'

Kyoul lifted his head weakly.

Graham went closer. Leanne had asked him to find out how Kyoul was. He tried to think of some questions suitable for a sick person. 'How's it going?' he whispered. 'Food OK? Hospital grub's usually bogging.'

'It is food,' Kyoul said in a low voice. 'And this hospital saved my life. When I left my village there were few medical services. You don't realize it, but here in the West you have so much.'

'I guess we have,' said Graham.

'You gave Leanne her phone?' Kyoul asked him.

'Yes,' said Graham. 'I went to her house yesterday and gave it to her.'

'Her parents? Did they find out about me?'

Graham shook his head. 'They'd gone out for the day.'

Kyoul waited a moment before saying, 'And she gave you the money?'

'Yes,' said Graham.

'Thank you,' said Kyoul. 'I thought you might not do it, even for the money.' He looked at Graham more intently. 'So why have you come here, to the hospital?'

'Leanne asked me to give you a message. She's worried you might tell them something and then you'll get deported. She says you've to hang on, say nothing, and she'll find a way to help you.'

'And you agreed to do this for her? For us?' said Kyoul. There was a note of caution in his voice. 'It must have been difficult for you to find me in the hospital. How did you do it? And why?'

'Someone's helping me,' said Graham. 'Someone we can trust,' he added quickly as he saw Kyoul's look of alarm. 'I came because Leanne was so worried about you. And – and she didn't have enough money on her yesterday, so she said she'd give me the rest when I saw her after I'd spoken to you again.'

'Ah yes.' Kyoul leaned back on the bed. 'Money.' Against the pillow his face was grey, the stubble of his beard a black smudge. 'Always, it comes down to money.'

'No,' said Graham. His face went red. 'It wasn't only that. Leanne was really upset, that's the reason I came, and . . . I was too. I wanted to make sure you were OK.'

'I'm sorry if I insulted you,' said Kyoul. 'I didn't mean it. It's just that I hear people say foreigners are leaving their own countries to take free benefits from others. Maybe some do, but it isn't the case for most of us.'

'I didn't know much about asylum seekers,' said Graham, 'but Leanne told us a bit about you.'

'Did she?' Kyoul looked wary. He pulled his pyjama jacket together. But not before Graham had seen the crisscrossing red and purple weals and small circular marks that covered his chest.

He frowned. 'What happened to you?'

Kyoul made a small movement of his head. 'I am a Muslim. In a country where it is no longer safe to be so. Religion. I believe that was the reason.' He sighed. 'But now I think there are those who will find any excuse to torture and kill. So it's good to have a scapegoat. Someone to blame for all your troubles.'

Torture – the word crashed around Graham's head. Kyoul had been *tortured*.

★ ★ ★

On his side of the curtain Joe was in difficulty. Two people, a man and a woman, were approaching Mr Sinclair's bed.

'There's my sister and her man,' Mr Sinclair said, looking beyond Joe's head. 'Coupla moaners, come to give me their weekly grudged visit.'

Joe scrambled to his feet. The sick he could deal with. These two might be a bit more on the ball.

'Haud on, son, haud on.' Mr Sinclair indicated for Joe to stay. 'This is Joe,' he said to the woman. 'Jimmy's boy. Remember Jimmy? We used to go to the dogs together.'

'Oh aye,' the woman said vaguely. 'I mind him . . . I think. How *is* your dad?'

'Och, he has his good days and his bad days,' replied Joe truthfully.

'Me too, son. Me too.' She sat down heavily. 'I'll take the weight off my feet here. I'm done in. This hospital's miles away for us and we don't have a car.' She scowled at her brother lying in the bed. 'Takes us hours to get here, by the way.'

'Aye. So it does,' said her husband. 'Standing at bus stops in the pouring rain.'

'It's no raining the day,' said Mr Sinclair. 'Is it, Joe?'

'That's no the point,' said the woman. 'Me and my man here, we're no as young as we used to be. And we cannae afford—'

'I need to go now,' Joe interrupted, shoving his own seat at her husband. '*I'll need to go*,' he said more loudly, hoping that Graham would hear him. '*I need to go* a message for my dad.' He flapped his hand at Mr Sinclair.

'You tell him I was asking for him,' said Mr Sinclair.

'Aye, mind and tell him,' said the woman.

'Aye. Right.' Joe backed off, trying to sustain the conversation, while keeping watch for any staff and an eye on the next bed. He wondered if Graham had heard him. There was no sign of any movement from behind the curtain. Then he spotted Graham walking up the ward towards the exit door.

'How did you sneak out so easily?' Joe asked him as he caught up with him on the staircase.

'Because Kyoul's bed's at the end of the ward, one side of the curtain is right next the toilets and there's two entrances to them,' said Graham. 'I walked through and came out on the far side of the ward.' He shook his head as he looked at Joe. 'I had to leave or you'd have been yapping on all day. You were getting carried away with your own story there. That poor man's in hospital, sick, and he gets you to put up with.'

'Listen, I made his day,' said Joe. 'Gave him something to talk about. And now that he's a mate of mine it means we can go back.'

Graham gave Joe a startled look.

'There's no way we're going back,' he said.

Chapter 26

In the City Hospital Kyoul rested his head against his pillows.

His heart was racing. Seeing the boy again had triggered his memory of Friday night. He closed his eyes and let the noise of the ward calm him. Even the sounds from the toilets and the sluice room close to his bed reassured him. Ordinary noises. Beyond his curtain he could hear a child laughing. People talking freely.

Freely.

Here everything was normal. A simple act of foolishness and he might now lose it all.

Friday night, on his way to meet Leanne, he'd been late. A trader who sometimes gave him work offered him extra to help unload some delivery vans in the evening. It meant he'd have a pound or two more. He would never allow Leanne to pay for anything. Not even a cup of coffee. So he'd agreed to do the job, and then rushed to meet her. Not wanting to keep her waiting, and knowing that they'd only have an hour together as her parents didn't allow her out late at night, he'd taken the short cut. Some older boys were gathered at the top of Reglan

Street. Kyoul had known right away that they were trouble. Angry energy spilled out from their faces. One grabbed his arm as he passed.

'Asylum seeker?'

Kyoul said nothing. Tried to go on.

The guy grinned at him. Lifted his shirt. Shown him the knife tucked in his belt.

'I'd run if I were you.'

In the hospital he sometimes cried out in the night. The man in the next bed, Peter Sinclair, would shout over, 'Press your call button, son.'

Kyoul always shook his head. 'No.'

He'd learned not to call for help. Many times he'd called out in his own language for mercy. It was a useless thing to do. It seemed to inflame his torturers. That's why he'd not struggled when the gang had dragged him from the close entrance and begun to beat him.

He'd said nothing. Tried to curl up, as he'd learned to do in the past, in order to protect himself against the boots and clubs. He'd not felt the knife go in. Only suddenly there was blood. The youths had run then. And he might have died in the street if the young boy had not telephoned for help.

He didn't know his name. Kyoul's eyes blinked open as he realized that he hadn't even asked the boy his name this second time they'd met. The boy wasn't all that much younger than he was. Yet older than Kyoul had been when war had come to his village. The war that had destroyed his life, killed his family, made his existence so unsafe: to be a Muslim male of a certain age meant that walking on the street was a hazard. He'd become a target. The last time he'd been interrogated one of his torturers spat in his face and told him that the next time they met would be the last.

He didn't have the resources to get out of his country. The people smugglers were highly organized. He couldn't pay their fee. One day he found himself walking west, following the setting sun. That night he slept in a ditch. The next day when he awoke he kept walking. Afterwards he couldn't recall making a decision to do this. But each day he walked in the same direction. In order to eat and pass through borders he'd had to do things he didn't want to think of now. Eventually he'd reached one of the big Red Cross camps. He'd been there for weeks when he met some relatives. They'd paid the smugglers to take all their family, but one of the children had died on the journey. They gave Kyoul the child's place, on the understanding that he was strictly on his own when they got into whatever country they were taken to.

He'd been bundled out of a lorry onto a motorway in the middle of the night. He'd no idea where he was. Saw the distant tower blocks and spires of a city, and once again began to walk.

He got into George Square on a cold morning in early spring. Hunger had made him feeble. He sat hunched on a bench and watched the city awake. Dawn unmasked the anonymous bulk of the buildings that framed the square and revealed their elegance. The perfume from the hyacinth beds was rising with the sun. Giddy with the intense blue of the flowers, the smell of the scent, the clarity of the air, Kyoul felt a happiness that he'd not experienced for a long time. As he began to know Scotland it reminded him of his own country. The way it had been once. A land of intense beauty, hard winters, triumphant greenery in spring. The city had so many parks. He spent lots of time there. It was how the city got its name, Leanne explained to him. Glas-gow – it meant 'the dear green place'. She told him the story of the symbols on the city coat of arms – the Bell, the Fish, the Bird and the Tree. He loved the parks: Alexandra Park, Linn Park, Victoria Park, the Winter Gardens at the People's Palace, Hogganfield Loch, Bellahouston, Kelvingrove, Rouken Glen. He liked the buildings too, the variety of the material, their colour – warm honey, pale cream, red sandstone, grey granite that picked up the clear northern light.

And the people.

His first day in the city.

There was a baker's shop on the corner of George Square. People were going in to buy food on their way to work. Kyoul went over. Stood in front of the window. A middle-aged woman came out of the shop. She glanced back as she saw him staring at the food on display. He'd been amazed at the variety. Trays of pies, fruit slices, cream cakes, buns, pastries, rolls stuffed full of meat, egg, tuna, cheese.

The woman walked close to him. Her eyes took in his worn shoes. She looked up, examined his face. Then she handed him the plastic carrier with her sandwiches and cake inside. 'You take that,' she said. 'I'll get myself some more.'

He hadn't thanked her. Couldn't speak. It was at that moment he'd fallen in love with the city.

And the girl, Leanne, with her face looking up at his. He thought he loved her too. He'd been determined to have no entanglements with anyone. Throughout his long journey he'd learned that he fared better on his own. But from the beginning she'd insisted on helping him. On showing him the city, almost as if she was discovering it for herself. He sensed her loneliness. She wasn't the kind of girl who went about in a group. Her interests were art and reading and classical music. They had a similarity in personality that brought them closer.

They rarely met at night. Her parents liked to know who she saw, who she was with. It was an hour stolen after school. In the library, one of the museums or art galleries, shopping on a Saturday, walking in the great greenhouse of the Kibble Palace.

What was Leanne doing now? he wondered. Was she even thinking of him? She must at least be concerned if she'd sent the boy back to see him in the hospital. But what could she do? He'd seen newspapers, watched television reports, knew the tone of public opinion. The smoothly spinning world had juddered, and never regained its balance. People were on their guard. Suspicion and uncertainty now stalked their lives. Would anyone help him?

Chapter 27

'So, are you coming for a game of football then?'

Joe asked Graham the question as they travelled on the bus back into the city centre from the hospital.

'You've brought your football gear with you anyway and we might as well get in some extra practice. I said I'd phone my uncle and let him know.'

'I suppose I could,' said Graham slowly. 'Who'll all be there?'

'My Uncle Desmond and some of his mates. They play fives every week. They're good and they know their stuff.'

'Your Uncle Desmond isn't Jammy's dad by any chance?' said Graham suspiciously.

'No,' Joe answered truthfully. He didn't let on that Desmond was really Jammy's uncle, Jammy's ma's brother, and therefore had some of the same loopy traits as all Jammy's family. 'Jammy always gets sent to visit his other granny on a Sunday,' Joe reassured Graham.

'I don't know,' said Graham. 'It was an Old Firm match yesterday. Your lot are bound to say something that'll annoy me.'

'Naw, naw,' said Joe. 'We'll go to my Auntie Kathleen's

to get changed. She lives in one of the new houses near Glasgow Green. Her husband, my Uncle Tommy, supports the Jags and she's dead against Rangers and Celtic. Says it causes too much trouble.' Joe didn't mention Desmond's actions of yesterday or that, as his granny always had Sunday dinner at his Auntie Kathleen's, most of the family dropped in to see her, so that by evening time the place would be full of his noisy relatives. 'Look, we're not all Ranger-hating, you know,' he added as Graham didn't answer.

'No?' said Graham.

'No,' said Joe.

'No prejudice against anyone?'

Joe thought for a moment. He decided that after yesterday he didn't see himself as the same kind of Celtic supporter as Desmond. 'It's not prejudice,' he said to Graham, 'when I support my team and you support yours.'

'So you'd say you were open-minded?' said Graham.

'Yes,' said Joe, wondering where this was leading.

'Supposing I was to tell you that I'm thinking of taking part in an Orange Walk next Saturday morning,' said Graham. 'What would you say?'

'I'd say you were having me on,' said Joe. 'What would you want to do that for?'

'My granda's in the Orange Lodge and he wants me to go with him.'

'But it's a daft thing to do,' said Joe.

'You've got Hibernian marches. I'll bet you don't think that's daft.'

'There's not as many of them,' said Joe. 'But I do think

they're daft. They're *all* mental' – he made a circle with his forefinger next the side of his head – 'folk that march up and down banging drums.'

'There's a good reason for ours. We do it to protect a principle,' said Graham. 'Everybody's got the right of free assembly, or should have. That's why the Orange Walks take place. My granda says his people had to fight to keep their religious freedom. That's what the Battle of the Boyne was all about. On the twelfth of July in sixteen ninety King Billy won that battle so that everybody could have their own faith and walk where they choose. Your people especially shouldn't object to someone standing up for what they believe.'

'Well, my dad says it was mainly to do with leaders wanting land and power, and abusing the good faith of ordinary folk,' said Joe. 'But through it all your lot made sure that Catholics got nothing. No church, no land, no houses, no jobs, no vote. You didn't want Catholics to live even.'

'That was ages ago,' said Graham. 'People don't think like that any more.'

'Some people do,' said Joe. He recalled his granny's remark to his dad about present-day bigotry. 'And your Orange Walks don't help. Why don't you just practise your religion quietly like everybody else? The Walks bring all the old stuff to the surface. It's dead offensive to hear people shouting things against you in public.'

'It's only the hangers-on that do that,' said Graham. 'What's offensive about the Orange Walk itself?'

'I've just told you,' said Joe. 'The way you do it sounds as though you're looking for a fight. You cause trouble marching about the streets dressed up in those stupid colours.'

'Stupid colours?' said Graham. 'One of the stripes in your Irish tricolour is orange. And I bet you don't even know why.' He waited, and as Joe didn't reply he went on, 'It's to represent the Orange people in Ireland. Chosen by the Irish themselves when they broke away from Britain.'

'No way!' said Joe. 'Who told you that?'

'My granda,' said Graham. 'And it's true. The Irish flag's green, white and orange. Green at one end. Orange at the other. And white in the middle as a symbol of peace between the two communities. So Orange men and women are supposed to have proper representation in all of Ireland.'

'That's the first I've ever heard of it,' said Joe. 'And I don't think there's many people in the Garngath would know that either.'

'Yeh,' said Graham. 'That's another thing. Those flags that were all over the Garngath yesterday. What is that all about?'

'What's *what* all about?' replied Joe tersely.

'You're in Scotland. Why have you got Irish flags hanging out your windows?'

'It's part of Celtic's tradition,' said Joe. 'It's why the football club was founded. To help the Irish poor in the city a hundred years ago. Celtic Football Club represented a community. Even though times have changed we don't turn our back on our history.'

'But you're *Scottish*.'

'I know that,' said Joe. 'But roots are important. Why

shouldn't we show where we're from? Other folk do. Anyway, my dad says we're all one people. Ireland and Scotland are mixed in with each other. He told me the *Scoti* were an Irish tribe who came over here and settled. The Scots are actually Irish. See? Anyway, why do you lot wave flags showing the Red Hand of Ulster?' Joe countered. 'Of *Ulster*,' he repeated. 'And at Ibrox Park you sing about King Billy on the Boyne in sixteen ninety. What's *that* got to do with Scotland?'

'It's part of the tradition,' said Graham.

'Well there you go,' said Joe. 'You've got your traditions and we've got ours.'

Both boys sat in silence until the bus went along Argyle Street into the city centre.

As they got off Joe nudged Graham. 'So, are you coming to play football then?'

Chapter 28

'We need to talk, you and I.'

Joe's Aunt Kathleen cornered him as he came out of the upstairs bathroom in her house. 'Your cousin Bernie phoned me. Said you wanted to tell me something.'

'Uh-uh. Don't think so,' said Joe, trying to sidestep his aunt.

'*Uh-uh*,' Kathleen mimicked him. 'I *do* think so.'

'No, really,' said Joe. 'I don't *want* to tell you anything.'

Kathleen smiled. 'But you're going to, aren't you? Mystery Man. Bernie says she's worried that you're getting into something way over your head.'

Joe grimaced. 'It's nothing. I went to visit someone at the City Hospital today and I'd to ask Bernie to help me find the ward. This person's in a bit of trouble. I wasn't involved,' he continued quickly, as he saw the expression on his aunt's face. 'I was only checking that he's OK for a friend, like. But Bernie made me promise I'd tell another adult or she'd phone my dad.' Joe gave Kathleen a pleading look. 'I don't want my dad bothered, he's been getting much better recently.'

'Is this "trouble" drug related?' said Kathleen.

'Definitely not.'

'What is it?'

'I'd be breaking someone else's trust if I told you.'

Kathleen shook her head. 'I'm not happy, Joe. I need you to tell me more. Bernie wouldn't have phoned me if she didn't think it was important. She has her hair done in the salon every month. The stories she tells us of the weirdos in hospitals would curl hair without me using rollers.' She laughed. 'And that's only the staff.'

'There you go then. Rest easy,' said Joe. 'Apart from Bernie I never spoke to any of the staff.'

'What's going on with this person you went to see?'

'I don't know exactly,' said Joe, 'and that's the truth. But I tell you what,' he went on as his aunt began to shake her head again, 'I'm in the middle of important football training just now. I promise I'll speak to my dad *after* our first real game takes place.'

'When's that?'

'The first leg's next Sunday. The youth team from Liverpool are coming up here to play Glasgow. I'm hoping to be picked for our team so I need to concentrate for the whole of this week. The coach will tell us who's been selected at the training on Friday.'

'A week?' said Kathleen. 'That's too long to wait.'

'I don't want anything to wreck my chances of being on the Glasgow City team. And,' Joe added, 'the guy in hospital's not going anywhere for at least a week.'

'The person whose trust you'd be breaking, are they criminals?'

‘Absolutely not!’ Joe laughed. ‘She’s just a girl.’

‘Less of the “just a girl”.’ Kathleen gave Joe a playful skelp on the ear.

‘I mean she’s nice . . . gentle.’ Joe looked sideways at his aunt. ‘They’re in love.’

‘Awww,’ said Kathleen, ‘now you’ve got me. I’m a sucker for a romance.’ She still didn’t move out of his way. ‘So what’s the problem?’

‘Religion mostly. Her family.’

‘Aw no!’ Kathleen groaned. ‘Tell me about it. When I got married to your Uncle Tommy he refused to become a Catholic. The trouble I had with your granny. She still doesn’t fully trust him – half expects him to up and leave me one day. You’re too young to remember the wedding. The families sat on opposite sides of the hall glowering at each other. Halfway through the night the band began playing *Simply the Best.* Desmond marched onto the floor and dragged his sister, your Aunt Rita, off because he didn’t want her dancing to a tune that Rangers fans sing. Would you believe it?’

‘Aye,’ said Joe, thinking of Desmond’s behaviour at yesterday’s game.

Kathleen regarded Joe for a few moments. ‘You promise you’ll tell your dad next weekend?’

‘Aye, OK,’ Joe said reluctantly.

His Aunt Kathleen took his arm as they went downstairs. ‘You know you’re my favourite nephew, don’t you? Your mum was my best pal at school, so I’ve got to look out for you. Make sure you’re OK. Apart from it being my sacred duty, she had a fearsome temper, your maw. If I let anything bad happen to you she'd come down from Heaven and thump me.'

'Yeh.' Joe pushed his aunt away laughing, wondering when it had happened that he could share a joke about his ma not being there any more. He looked at his dad's face as he went into the kitchen. Would *he* ever be able to laugh about losing her?

'I'm trying to persuade your wee pal here to stay for dinner.' Joe's Aunt Rita had befriended Graham, who was wedged between the fridge and the archway leading to the dining part of the main room, trapped by her bulk.

Graham shook his head. 'I can't.'

'Why not?'

Graham knew that Joe would think he was being snobby, refusing an invitation to stay and eat with his family. But he wasn't. The smell of cooking in Joe's Aunt Kathleen's kitchen smelled better than what would be getting brewed up in his own. But he knew his mum would ask tons of questions if he phoned her. 'I just can't,' he repeated.

'I'll give you a lift when I'm taking Joe home later,' Joe's Uncle Tommy spoke up.

'Don't harass the boy,' said Kathleen. 'Maybe he doesn't want to.'

'But I do.' The words came out before Graham could stop them. And he did. Despite being a bit wary of Desmond, whose play was quite physical and whose face, he noticed, had fresh bruises, he'd learned a great deal about collective intelligent play in this afternoon's conversation, and during the kick-about on Glasgow Green. Joe's family talked football and Graham enjoyed listening. His own dad was interested in what he did, never failing to ask about his football training, but he was more of a golfer. He could debate on birdies and eagles but couldn't argue the merits of a defender versus a winger. In Joe's family they could discuss individual and team skills, plus moments from the great games. Could tell you that it had been a chip back from Morgan that had allowed Jordan to head in the goal that had taken Scotland through to the World Cup Finals in West Germany. They had a grasp of tactics and seemed to know almost as much history as his Granda Reid.

'It's just that my mum . . .' Graham faltered. He'd sound like a wimp if he said his mum worried about him.

'I'll talk to your dad,' said Joe's dad. 'Put your phone number there.' He gave Graham a pencil and notepad that was lying on the work surface. 'Use your phone, Kathleen?'

'Sure, Joseph, help yourself.'

'I'll tell your dad where you are and that we'll give you a run home to your door in a couple of hours.'

'Dad' – Joe followed his dad into the hall – 'see, when you're talking to Gregory's dad . . .'

'Yes?'

'Could you call him Graham?'

'His dad's name is Graham?'

'Naw. I don't know his dad's name.'

'Why am I calling him Graham then?'

'It's no him I want you to call Graham.'

'Who *do* you want me to call Graham?'

'Gregory.'

'Son,' said Joe's dad, 'I haven't a clue what you're talking about.'

'Look,' Joe snapped. 'See that boy in there having his ear dinged by Aunt Rita? His name is Graham. But when he's here we call him Gregory.'

'Why?'

'We just do. OK?'

Joe's dad pursed his lips. 'OK,' he said slowly. 'I think . . .'

'Dad, pay attention! You've got to get this right. When Graham is here his name is Gregory. When he's at home his name is Graham. So when you speak to his dad on the phone you call him Graham. Not his dad, you understand? It's Gregory you'll call Graham.'

Joe returned to the kitchen and his dad picked up the phone. As he began to dial the number Joe's dad spoke softly to himself.

'Is it any wonder I suffer from mental illness?'

When he returned to the dining room Joe glanced up with a questioning frown. His dad grinned back.

'Your dad was telling me he's a dentist,' he addressed Graham, who was now seated at the dinner table. 'He said that when he qualified he was with a surgery in the East End before he moved across the city. Turns out it was quite close to Joe's granny's hairdressing shop. It's a small world, isn't it? It also turns out he must have been at Glasgow University when I was finishing my doctorate.'

'You're a doctor?' Graham couldn't keep the surprise out of his voice.

There was an awkward pause. Graham was aware everyone was looking at him.

'That's right,' said Joe's dad. 'I've a PhD in political history.' He smiled at Graham across the table. 'Help yourself to some potatoes, Gregory.'

Chapter 29

'That ref yesterday must've have been a mason.'

Graham kept his eyes on his plate. He might have known that, despite Joe's assurances, his family wouldn't be able to get through the day without some reference to yesterday's game. Dinner was over and Rita was talking to her brother Desmond.

'Bigoted b, so he was,' Desmond agreed.

'You're right there, Desmond,' said Rita. 'Jammy and I watched it on the telly together. We saw him, plain as day, giving one of those funny handshakes to the linesman.'

Graham gasped. He couldn't stop himself. The replays he had watched proved that the breaks had all gone Celtic's way.

'Aye, you wouldn't believe it, would you, Gregory?' Desmond had misinterpreted Graham's reaction. 'But that's what goes on. Pure prejudice, so it is.'

'Enough,' said Kathleen. 'I've told you lot before. When you have dinner at my house there's no post-mortem on Celtic games. Football annoys me. It causes too much bad feeling, and anyway Tommy supports Partick Thistle.'

'Aw *c'mon*,' said Desmond, 'even a Jags supporter has to admit that was never a goal in the first half. We would've won the game but for that. Did you see it, Gregory? What did you think?'

'Aye,' Joe chimed, affecting a serious, attentive manner. 'What did *you* think, Gregory?'

Graham stared hard at Joe. Then he smiled and opened his eyes wide. 'I think' – he spoke slowly – 'that you're right. The ref *was* biased. It was blatantly obvious. No matter what the opposition says. The better team was robbed in the end.'

'Once again they did the dirty on us. We were the best team on the park. By a mile,' said Desmond.

'*We* were,' said Graham. 'Def-in-itely.' He shot Joe a look of triumph.

When dinner was over Joe and Graham sat on at the dining table and began to draw out sketches of line formations while the adults tried to persuade Kathleen's husband Tommy to sing a song.

'*Danny Boy*. It's my favourite song,' said Joe's granny. 'You've got a lovely voice, Tommy. And,' she added in a placating tone, 'it's one both sides can sing with no offence to either.'

'Not *Danny Boy*,' protested Desmond. 'I'd rather hear *The Croppy Boy*.'

'None of that,' said Kathleen. 'This is a peaceable neighbourhood.'

'Oh I see,' said Desmond. 'You've changed your tune since you've gone up in the world.'

'I'm no going to annoy folk. They don't annoy me.'

'This is *my* culture,' said Desmond. 'This is *my* music.'

'Aye, but this is *my* house,' said Kathleen, 'and I'll fling you out if you start with any of your rebel songs.'

'Gaun yourself, Kathleen,' said her husband, Tommy.

'We shouldn't stop rebelling,' said Desmond, 'until we are truly free.'

'You're free to leave any time you like, Desmond,' said Kathleen.

'That's not what I mean.' Desmond glared at her. 'What I'm talking about here is the situation where we are still being discriminated against. For instance, I'll have you know, I could not become the next King of Britain.'

'You're right there, Desmond,' said Kathleen. 'You could not.'

'And,' Desmond went on, ignoring her sarcasm, 'from now until July a load of loonies can march all over this city chanting things about Catholics, and we have to shut up and listen to it.'

'The Orangemen don't chant anything,' said Joe's dad. 'And although, personally, I think they're misguided, they say they're not aware of any unpleasantness in the crowds that turn up.'

'That'll be right!' said Rita with heavy scorn. 'If they don't know what goes on around them when they pass by, then they must have those wee bowler hats that they sometimes wear pulled all the way down over their eyes and ears.'

'They're trying to let us know our place,' said Desmond.

'Or perhaps keep their own place,' said Joe's dad mildly.

'Maybe there's more to it than that,' said Tommy. 'Perhaps the powers that be have got it all worked out to give the mob an outlet for their aggression. All the cheering and shouting encourage men to think they're a united brotherhood.'

'I'll say yes to united Irishmen,' said Desmond.

'The United Irishmen were the original rebels,' said Joe's dad, 'formed by women and men – like the patriot Wolfe Tone, for example – who were of different faiths.'

'Yeh, faith,' said Desmond. 'Faith of our fathers. They tried to crush that out of us. But we resisted, *In spite of dungeon, fire, and sword . . .*'

He held his hands high in the air and began to sing:

'Faith of our fathers! Holy Faith!
We will be true to thee till death,
We will be true to thee till death.'

'Gie's a break, Desmond,' said Kathleen.

'If you don't have your faith' – Desmond pointed his finger at her – 'you have nothing. Nothing.'

'When did you last go to church?' Joe's granny asked him.

'That's a private matter between myself and my Maker,' declared Desmond.

'I wish your singing was an all,' said Joe's granny.

'You don't have to be flocking to church every week to be a true believer,' said Rita. 'It's what's in your heart that counts.'

'Aye, right,' scoffed Kathleen. 'See all these folk that only go to the Chapel twice a year? Hypocrites! Turn up on Ash Wednesday to get their ashes so they can walk about the town with the smit on their forehead. And on Christmas Eve they stagger up to Midnight Mass after the pubs shut to stand at the back half cut, and then go up to see the crib and keel over beside the baby Jesus.'

'I fulfil my duties,' said Desmond.

'Going to Parkhead during the football season does not fulfil one's religious obligations,' said Tommy, in a solemn voice. 'Even if one also does attend the away games.'

'Desmond was in church for my wedding,' said Rita. '*And* he stayed all through the service. Not like some I could mention, who skipped out early to get to the hotel afore everybody else, so they could get tore into the whisky and the sherry and the bucks fizz laid out for the guests arriving. And,' she sniffed, 'they weren't from *my* side of the family, by the way. Our Desmond stayed right to the end of the Nuptial Mass, didn't you, Desmond?'

'Aye, I did.'

'Rita' – Joe's Aunt Kathleen laughed – 'you were married over *twenty* year ago.'

'Point of principle,' said Desmond. 'Point of principle.'

'Yes,' said Joe's dad, 'that's why it bemuses me that people who don't practise their faith get all fired about it.'

'For some people it's an excuse to have a rammy,' said Kathleen.

'Naw it's no,' said Desmond.

'Aye it is,' said Kathleen.

'Naw it's no.'

'Desmond, you know it is.'

'Are you callin me a liar?' Desmond made as if to stand up. 'I'm no easily riled, but if I get to my feet . . .'

'If you do get to your feet, Desmond, go into the kitchen and put the kettle on, will you?' said Joe's granny.

'That's another one of the things he hasn't done for twenty year,' said Kathleen.

All the women started laughing.

It's reality TV, thought Graham from his vantage point at one end of the room. He'd heard programme makers were always keen for new ideas. If only he'd thought to bring a camcorder with him. He could have made a fortune.

Joe, obviously accustomed to scenes like this, ignored his relatives and went on talking tactics and drawing diagrams. Graham tried to concentrate on what Joe was saying, but when the adults' conversation turned to the Orange Walk due to take place next Saturday his whole body tensed.

'Some of the marchers are no bad looking,' said Kathleen, smiling. 'We stood and watched them go past the shop last year. One of them gave me the eye.'

'Aye, the *evil* eye,' said Rita. 'He probably thought you were going to try to cross the street in front of them. You'd have seen how much he fancied you if you'd tried that.'

'No, he was OK. If he hadn't had all his regalia on he might have been passable.'

'With or without the regalia, I think you can tell them

apart,' said Desmond. 'You just need to look at them. And you can tell.'

'The way they say they can tell us?' asked Joe's dad in an amused voice.

'Oh, I agree with them there,' said Joe's granny. 'I can tell our own. I mean, look at Joe's new pal there from the football training. Wee Gregory.'

It took Graham several seconds before he realized they were talking about him.

'You can tell he's Donegal bred,' Joe's granny went on. 'Give me his second name and I could probably place him to the exact village. He has the look of the black Irish.'

The black Irish? Graham kept his face blank.

Joe's dad leaned forward. 'In case you're wondering, *Gregory*,' he said to Graham, 'the black Irish are the Irish who are descended from the survivors of the ships of the Spanish Armada, part of which was wrecked off the west coast of Ireland. They intermarried with the local population, whose subsequent offspring had distinctively more sallow skin and dark hair.'

'Right,' said Graham. His voice was neutral, but the look he directed at Joe was pure panic.

Joe shrugged his shoulders as if to say, 'It's nothing to do with me.'

'If your ancestors are from the Emerald Isle,' Joe's dad continued, 'you can probably trace your lineage to Spanish nobility on one side, while on the other side you'll be a direct descendant of the High Kings of Ireland.'

'See, you're having a wee joke there, Joseph,' said

Desmond. 'But your ma's right. What's bred in the bone comes out in the blood. Look at the boy. You can tell. Name like Gregory an all. Dead give away, that.'

'Do you think so?' Joe's dad laughed.

'*Lovely* name, Gregory,' said Rita. 'Jammy told me your ma called you after a pope, didn't she, son?'

Almost certainly not, Graham thought silently. He stood up. He had to get out of the room.

Joe looked at Graham. He flicked his glance towards the door. Graham moved his head in a very slight nod.

Rita saw him standing up. 'Where're you going, son?'

'Need a pee,' Graham mumbled.

Chapter 30

Later that evening Graham had not taken two steps inside his house when his mum was beside him.

'Where are the people who brought you home?'

'Er – they drove away,' said Graham.

'Did they not think to wait to say hello?'

'They were in a hurry.'

'They were not.' Graham's dad laughed. 'You got them to drop you at the end of the street so that you wouldn't have to introduce us.'

Graham blushed.

His dad put his hand on his shoulder. 'Did the same thing myself when I was your age. Parents are *so* embarrassing, aren't they?'

Graham gave his dad a grateful look. He was taking the pressure off.

But his mum was not to be deterred. 'Tell us all about this new friend of yours,' she said.

'Not now, Mum. I'm really tired and I've got things to sort out for school tomorrow.' Graham went into the lounge and rummaged through the Sunday papers, looking for the sports section.

'I don't recall you mentioning this boy Joe before,' said his mum, following him into the room. 'He's not a pupil at your school, is he?'

Graham shook his head.

'So . . . what school *does* Joe go to?'

Graham looked straight at his mum. 'I never asked him,' he said truthfully.

Under her son's direct stare Graham's mother's face went slightly pink.

'Your dad and I are concerned for you. I don't want to be overprotective, but—'

'I was just playing football with a friend, and he asked me to his aunt's house for dinner. That's all.'

'And did you have a nice time?' his mum asked.

'Ye-*es*!' said Graham. He grabbed a handful of the Sunday papers and his rucksack and went quickly upstairs to his room.

He flung the bundle of stuff onto his bed and sat down. He *was* tired. He'd been telling his mum the truth when he'd told her that. And it wasn't just his muscles with playing so much football over the last few days; his brain was churning too.

It had been a heavy weekend. First the excitement of scoring the goal at football training and maybe increasing his chances of being selected for the team. Then the horrible incident in Reglan Street, with all the further complications of helping Leanne by going to the hospital to give Kyoul her message. Graham felt his mind dip when he thought about Kyoul. Remembering the torture marks on the Kyoul's body made him queasy. He hadn't wanted to go to the hospital, but was glad he had. To see

Kyoul safe made him feel better. He could understand why Leanne had wanted them to go and talk to him to make sure he was OK. Although it had been Joe who had done most of the work for that, blagging his way into the hospital ward.

Joe . . . Graham had never met anyone quite like Joe before – someone totally different from him in every way. Yet he liked him. He liked Joe's dad too, now that he'd spoken to him a bit more, and his Aunt Kathleen. She was less uptight than the other adults, especially when they'd been talking about Saturday's Orange Walk. She'd a wicked sense of humour and chatted away to him when cooking the dinner, and Graham found himself talking to her quite easily. It was only Jammy and Desmond who made him uncomfortable. There was no doubt that Desmond was brilliant at football and good at coaching. But his voice, his manner, the bruises on his face and his talk at dinner made Graham think that he was one of those people his parents might not want him to be associated with.

On top of all that, there was the pressure from his granda and his granda's friends to take part in their local Orange Walk next week. When Sadie had spoken to him in the kitchen Graham felt ashamed that he hadn't yet agreed to go. So why was it then, when he'd first told Joe about it, he'd felt uncomfortable that he was even thinking of taking part? He almost wished that his parents weren't leaving it up to him to make the decision.

Graham picked up the newspapers and looked for the sports section to read the write-ups from Saturday's game. Rangers should never have allowed Celtic to get that equalizer in the second half. Team tactics were lacking, said this reporter. Graham thumbed his way through the rest. There was a report about some trouble afterwards. An injured person had been taken to A&E. What had begun as a minor clash of rival groups chucking potatoes at each other had escalated into hard violence.

Graham had seen the Rangers fans at the front throwing potatoes onto the pitch at Parkhead. He'd thought it was really funny. After all, as his granda said, Celtic supporters were always singing about the Irish Famine. The potatoes were a good wind-up. But it said that an old man had to have stitches in his head. Graham threw the newspaper on his bed. Would it never stop? Both clubs were trying to do something positive, running anti-bigotry campaigns and banning abusive fans. At Ibrox Park, the Rangers football ground, and Parkhead, the home of Celtic, sectarian songs were banned. But some people wouldn't listen. It was as though the actual football wasn't the reason they came to the games. They soured it by linking it with religious prejudice.

Religion should help you lead a better life, that's what his parents told him. His mum went to church most Sundays, his dad often went with her. They never pressured him to go with them so sometimes he went too. They passed a Catholic church on the way. There were always people going in or coming out. Everybody smiled and said hello. So how come fights happened about religion? Why couldn't they live side by side happily all the time? Why was there a problem with Kyoul and Leanne being together? Was it never going to stop?

Graham pushed the pile of newspapers to one side. As he did so he caught sight of an article in the main news section.

His heart bucked in his chest.

From the top of a page Kyoul's face was staring out at him.

Above the photograph the headline read:

DO YOU KNOW THIS MAN?

Chapter 31

Graham's hands shook as he spread the newspaper out on his bed.

> **DO YOU KNOW THIS MAN?**
> The police are still anxious to establish the identity of this young man, who was attacked in the city centre on Friday night. They would like to speak to the person they know was at the scene of the crime, a boy with dark hair wearing a grey sweat-shirt, to come forward to help with their enquiries. The injured man, known only as Kyoul, is suffering from amnesia and is recovering in hospital. He may be of eastern European origin. If you have any information please contact Central Police Station.

Sickness rose in Graham's throat.

Anyone who read that might know it was him! And it sounded even more as if he'd been actively involved in the attack. He tried to be calm and think the way Joe did. Joe, who seemed not to panic about anything. Graham read the description of himself again. 'A boy'. It could be any boy, couldn't it? 'Dark hair and grey sweatshirt'. There must be loads of boys with dark hair and grey sweatshirts. Graham began to reason things out as he packed his rucksack for school and got ready for bed. He was safe, he told himself. No one would suspect that he was the boy mentioned in the newspaper. The police couldn't have enough information to find him or they would have already called at the house. If Kyoul decided to tell the police what happened then he didn't know Graham's name or anything about him. And his parents must have read this and they weren't knocking on his bedroom door to question him.

All he had to do was meet up with Joe tomorrow after school and go and tell Leanne that Kyoul was OK. Once that was done he would have nothing more to do with any of it.

Downstairs in Graham's house his mum was talking to his dad.

'Why do you think Graham was so abrupt with me tonight?' she asked.

'As boys get older they don't like chatting with their parents, darling. It's a fact of life.'

'He's been a bit preoccupied the last few days,' said Graham's mum. 'D'you think this is the start of his difficult teenage years?'

'You *were* quizzing him a bit, pet,' said Graham's dad.

'But we need to know where he's been and who with. We don't want him hanging around with the wrong sort.'

'Liz,' said Graham's dad, 'you knew that this football training wasn't individual-school based. The head teacher sent letters to every parent explaining the project. All the big cities in Britain have signed up for it – Manchester, Edinburgh, Birmingham, London, Liverpool. It's one of the government's initiatives to improve sports skills, encourage youngsters to keep fit, keep them out of mischief, and give the cities of Britain an opportunity to bring communities together and take pride in their youth. The whole idea is that it would be an *all*-city team, no one area preferred over the other. The trials are open to kids from anywhere in the city. It was great that Graham was chosen from his school to take part and I think it's good for him to get out with lads his own age from other parts of the city.'

'What's your point?' asked Graham's mum, bristling.

'He has to mix with people from different backgrounds. This boy Joe can't possibly be at Graham's school. He lives miles away.'

'Quite a few parents from outside this area try to get their children into Graham's school. Joe could have been a placing request.'

'It's not likely though, is it? To follow through a placing request you need to have the means to do it. That's the insidious aspect about any kind of so-called "choice". Unless you have money there *is* no choice. You read the newspapers. Glasgow has some of the most deprived areas in Britain. I've worked in these places, I've seen what that sort of environment can do to self-esteem. People get desperate and angry. It can lead to violence. Deprivation,' said Graham's dad. 'Deprivation, and all that goes with it, is what really divides this city.'

'I don't want Graham making unsuitable friends.'

'Graham will be fine. Joe seems a good lad, and I was talking to his dad on the telephone earlier. He sounds like a nice man.'

'Where they live,' said Graham's mum, 'it's such a different part of the city from this.'

'Is that the real reason you're worried?'

'What?'

'It's the "other side", isn't it?'

'I don't know what you mean by that.'

'It's because they stay in the Garngath, isn't it?'

'It's not a very nice place,' said Graham's mother.

'Not everyone can afford to live in a nice place, Liz.'

'It's got a reputation.'

'*Parts* of it have got a reputation. Parts of every area in this city have a reputation. There are streets not far from here that I wouldn't walk along in daylight, far less in the dark.'

'It's not the same. Things are different over there.'

'You mean *they* are different,' said Graham's dad. 'You're talking about the people who live there, aren't you? Liz, you know my sister married a Catholic. It might surprise your family but when her children were born they didn't have a tail and two horns.'

'I know lots of Catholics. Two of the lawyers I work with are Catholics.'

'Yes, but they're not Catholics who live in the Garngath. You know as well as I do, in Scotland, there's Catholics, and there's Catholics. Scotland had Catholics before Irish immigration took place. But the old

Catholic Scots from earlier days are almost forgotten about. It's the *Irish* Catholic influence that sets some people's teeth on edge. And your family are from Bridgebar. There's a conflict there.'

'My family are not prejudiced.'

'Your family are from an area with strong connections to Ulster Protestantism, and are very . . . partisan in their beliefs. Your father is a deeply caring person and worked hard all his life. I love John dearly. And I respect him for how he put his own job on the line when he fought against the closure of the shipyards. But, and I quote, "There are times when he can be a narrow-minded sectarian racist." '

'Don't talk about my father like that!'

Graham's dad came over and sat beside his wife. 'It was you I was quoting, Liz. When Graham was a very small boy and you heard your dad trying to persuade him to march in one of the Junior Orange Walks, those were your very words.'

Graham's mum was close to tears. 'Graham's our only child. And he'll always be our only child. You know all the problems I had having him. Graham's my son. A mother has a duty to protect her son. I'm only doing what I think is right.'

Graham's dad put his arms around his wife and held her tight.

Chapter 32

Graham arrived at school on Monday morning to find a special assembly had been called.

The head teacher announced that there was a possibility that someone in the school had been involved in an incident in the city on Friday night. A younger boy and an older boy had been attacked by a gang. The older boy had been stabbed. The police wanted to speak to the younger boy, who had run away from the City Hospital.

A witness had stated that the younger boy had been wearing a school sweatshirt reported to be grey. It may or may not have had a coloured stripe on it. Everyone could see that their school sweatshirt was grey with a purple edging. The boy who was wounded seemed to speak with an eastern European accent. If anyone had any information about the incident could they please come forward?

Graham's pulse rate was notching up megabeats but he tried to affect the bored inattention that the rest of his classmates were showing.

'Why are the police looking around out here? It's obvious where they should be asking their questions,' said one of Graham's friends at break time. 'They should be questioning people in the schools where they've got most of the asylum seekers.'

'Yeh, I don't see why we're getting grief about it,' protested another of the boys in Graham's class. 'My dad says it's always teenage Asian boys that get involved in stuff like that.'

'It's nothing to do with them,' said Graham.

'How do *you* know?'

'They said the guy was from eastern Europe. I think that's what gave me the clue,' said Graham sarcastically. 'Like, Asia – over there. Europe – up here. Du-uh?'

'Aye, aye,' said the other boy. 'That's not the point. They're different from us, see? Don't have our background, our way of thinking. Don't look the same even.'

Graham was still anxious when he left school that afternoon.

At one point during the day he'd thought of speaking to one of his teachers whom he knew he could trust. Only the fact that he should let Joe know first stopped him. He thought of how bad it would be for Joe's dad if the police began questioning Joe.

When the final bell went Graham didn't walk home as usual. Instead he caught a bus into the city. This time he stayed on until he was in the city centre, where the streets were familiar to him from shopping trips and outings with his parents. He got off in Queen Street and was soon outside the ornate building that housed the Gallery of Modern Art, known to everyone in Glasgow as GOMA. Joe was waiting next to the statue of the man on the horse with the traffic cone on his head. Graham knew it was the Duke of Wellington and that his horse was called Copenhagen. The reason he remembered was because his dad had told him one day last year when they had been driving past the GOMA, and the very next week it had come up in an inter-schools quiz question. His dad had also said that every so often there was a letter to the paper saying how scandalous it was that every weekend some late-night reveller climbed up and stuck a traffic cone on the duke's head. And although it was always removed, by the following weekend it was back again. Some people thought it was the same cone. Complainers moaned on about the lack of respect and said that the police should arrest whoever was doing it. But everybody reckoned that it was never the same person. It had become a Glasgow tradition, like changing the position of the spectacles on Donald Dewar's statue. More a statement of affection than vandalism. At least it wasn't ignored like most statues of the famous and not so famous.

Graham told Joe about the newspaper article and the announcement at his school. 'The police must have been speaking to the teachers,' said Graham. 'They're onto something.'

'They were at my school too,' said Joe.

'What!' Graham exclaimed. 'How did they find out you were involved? Was it your Cousin Bernie? Did she tell the police we'd been asking about Kyoul?'

'Calm down,' said Joe. 'Bernie is family. She would never do that. If she felt obliged to say anything more she'd have spoken to my dad or my granny.'

'Really?' Graham relaxed.

'Our school has grey sweatshirts too,' explained Joe. 'I asked our school janny and he told me the polis are going to every school whose uniform is grey sweatshirts. We've a maroon stripe, not purple like yours, but I'll bet the witness wasn't sure about that.'

'I was pretty freaked out,' said Graham. 'Thought I might be called to a line-up or something.'

'You might still.'

'What? Might still what?'

'Get called to the head's office.'

'Why?'

'Think about it. Your teachers know that you go into the city centre for football practice on a Friday. They might think that you saw something on your way home.'

'Except that's not the way I'm supposed to go home.'

'That's even better then. Don't you let on to anyone that you took a short cut. It puts you in the clear. Anyway,' Joe went on, 'if they follow up on the asylum seekers lead they'll talk to the immigrant kids. The whole thing'll take them weeks, months even. They're onto plums with that one.'

The two boys went inside the GOMA to find the library café, where they had arranged to meet Leanne. 'This is one mad gallery,' said Joe.

'You come here often?' Graham jibed.

'Used to. Nearly every week with my ma when I was younger. They hold interactive sessions on a Saturday morning. It's free and you just turn up. I like it in here. The staff are friendly. Not snotty, like some places. Tell you loads of things about the artists. Explain the stuff to you. Because it's modern, like, and they think you might not get it.'

Graham looked at the nearest exhibit as they went through into the museum. It was an enormous complicated construction of wire and metal, in the middle of which sat a garden gnome perched on a bicycle seat. 'I can see why some of it might need to be explained,' he said.

'There was an artist working here once,' said Joe. 'Stayed for days and days building this huge exhibit. Made up of a burned-out car and thousands of newspapers. They cleared practically the whole ground floor for him to do it. Me and my ma came every day after school. He would stop and talk to us. Brilliant, so it was.'

'Right,' said Graham. It seemed to be that every time he was getting a handle on what Joe was like he got wrong-footed. He followed Joe in the direction of the café and tried to outstare the garden gnome as he passed by.

Chapter 33

Leanne was already waiting for them.

At first Graham and Joe didn't recognize her. She looked nearer their age dressed in her school uniform – a dark blazer and plaid pleated skirt. Her eyes looked strained, as if she'd been crying or hadn't slept well. They got some drinks and sat in a corner to talk.

'Kyoul's OK,' said Graham.

He saw the effect of his words on Leanne. She relaxed immediately.

'Thank God,' she said.

'My cousin,' said Joe, 'the one that's the nurse – she said the doctors in the hospital think Kyoul can't remember anything and also that he can't speak much English.'

Leanne smiled. 'Kyoul can speak English really well.'

'So he's got them well fooled,' said Joe. 'He says nothing and acts confused all the time. They seem to believe him because of the shock he must've suffered. But Graham saw him and he's doing fine.'

'You're sure?' Leanne looked at Graham. 'Did he speak to you?'

Graham nodded. 'They'd to give him blood, but he's

OK.' He recalled the marks on Kyoul's chest. 'He's safe now,' he said reassuringly. 'He was able to talk to me.'

Leanne's face crumpled in relief. She began to cry. 'I'm sorry,' she said. 'I'm sorry. Only, I've been so worried, and I couldn't talk to anyone about it.'

'He's OK,' Joe repeated. 'On the mend and that.'

Leanne rubbed at her eyes. 'I've brought the rest of your reward money,' she said. 'Here.' She took two envelopes from her inside blazer pocket. She put one on the table. 'Here's the money you were promised, and there's some extra notes inside.'

'Extra?'

'Yes.' Leanne spoke quickly. 'I'd like you to take this other envelope to Kyoul.' She placed the second envelope on the table.

'No way!' said Joe. He took the envelope with the money and handed it to Graham. He didn't touch the other one. 'It's over. We've done all we can.'

'Let me explain,' said Leanne. She went on quickly before they could refuse. 'After you left on Saturday I thought about Kyoul. About his life. I saw how selfish I'd been. He needs help and in a way I've been stopping him getting it. He earns a little money here and there and has me for company so he is happy, because what he came from was so awful. But it isn't right. He can't go on like that. On Saturday afternoon I went to the library and they gave me the names of various organizations like the Refugee Council. Some have telephone help lines. And Glasgow has set up asylum drop-in centres all over the city. He could meet people from his own country and the staff there would help him. I've written them all down on a piece of paper inside this envelope. You could give it to Kyoul. Tell him if he doesn't want to phone them I'll do it for him. He could get advice. It might stop him being deported.'

'Why did Kyoul come here if he knew he wouldn't be allowed in?' said Joe.

'He hoped he would,' said Leanne. She looked from one boy to another. 'People don't know the awful reasons why asylum seekers come to Britain or what they've gone through to get here. I didn't until I met Kyoul. Then I began to read up on it.'

Like me, thought Graham, remembering his Internet search last Friday night.

Joe didn't reply. His dad knew about things like this, politics and foreign news, but he'd never paid attention. Joe lived and breathed football. Nothing much else interested him. Though he did remember his dad once describing how the Irish had been treated by some when they'd first come to Scotland. 'Send them back,' people had said. 'Don't let them in.' His father said the Irish had been starving. Starving to death. They'd had to go anywhere they could earn money in order to eat.

'I'm begging you to take this to Kyoul.' Leanne held out the other envelope again.

Joe shook his head.

'Please. Only this one more time. I'll pay you extra money.'

Joe glanced at Graham. 'We can't.'

'Kyoul needs this information,' Leanne pleaded. 'What if he's forced to return to his own country?'

Joe shook his head again.

'How much do you want?' Leanne asked desperately. 'I've got friends I can borrow money from.'

'It's not that,' Joe protested. He looked at Graham, who had said nothing for several minutes.

'I'll do it,' said Graham.

Joe sat back and stared at Graham.

Leanne too appeared startled. 'It'll take a couple of days for me to get the cash but I *will* give you more money.'

Graham handed Leanne the envelope containing the money. 'I'm not doing it for the money,' he said.

Joe blinked. 'You're not?' he said.

'No.' Graham looked at him steadily. 'There's more to it than the money.' He picked up the second envelope from the table. 'I'll take this to Kyoul. It'll be a few days before I can get to the hospital again. I've got supported study tomorrow when school finishes, and another football session on Wednesday evening. But I'll go on Thursday afternoon. We can meet on Friday and I'll tell you how I got on. I've got time to see you after our football training.'

Leanne looked as though she might cry again. She swallowed a few times, then she leaned over and touched Graham on the cheek. 'Thank you,' she said.

'What was that all about?' Joe asked as he and Graham left the GOMA. '*There's more to it than the money?*'

'I didn't tell you this,' said Graham. 'Yesterday when I spoke to Kyoul in the hospital I saw his chest and arms . . .' He frowned and looked at Joe. 'He'd been tortured. I mean, like, *really* tortured. It keeps coming into my mind. I go to all those action movies and spy thrillers, and you see things on telly, but I've never met anyone who has actually been tortured. It was – was . . .' Graham ran out of words. He experienced again the slipping, sliding feeling he'd felt inside when he'd looked at Kyoul's body and raised his gaze to his eyes. Seen the flayed, fearful look, the shadows in their depths.

'Scary,' said Joe.

'Terrifying. And – and close. That's what's most scary. This happened in central Europe. I mean, my mum and dad have been on holiday there. It was the same as here practically. The people lived the way we do. Normal. And then it all changed. And people did things to each other. I don't know why but they did. Ordinary people. It was ordinary people, like neighbours, who did that to Kyoul.'

'My dad says that war changes people.'

'I also read up about refugees on the Internet,' said Graham. 'One website showed children trying to live in bombed-out buildings. It gave you facts on human rights abuses in some countries. No wonder people try to escape. Some of them are doctors and teachers and they're not allowed to work when they get here. Their life is just a big fat zero.'

They walked on for a bit, then Joe said, 'From where I live I can see the high flats where lots of the asylum seekers have been placed. They've had two suicides over there in the last year.'

'I spoke to a refugee boy in our school this afternoon,' said Graham. 'We don't have very many asylum seekers, but when they arrived, the teachers did projects with us so we'd share information and experiences. But I never listened *properly* to what they were saying. This boy told me why his family left his own country. His father worked in education and he spoke out for civil rights. One day men came to their house. They killed his father and his older brother while they were having dinner. Beat them and shot them. Right in front of him and his mother and his baby sister. An uncle paid smugglers to help them escape. They'd to leave everything behind. Everything. He and his mum and his wee sister walked every night for hours and hours, across half the world. During the day they were put in a hole in the ground to hide. His sister has asthma. One night the smugglers threatened to kill her because she couldn't stop coughing. They've been waiting two years since they got here to see if they can stay. His mum never goes out. She hardly speaks to anyone.' Graham spoke the next sentence fiercely. 'That's why I'm not doing it for the money.'

Joe sighed. 'I suppose you'll be wanting me to go with you again?'

'You look after the envelope with the information until Thursday,' said Graham. 'I don't want my parents to find it. My mum can be a real nuisance sometimes. She comes in my room all the time to tidy up and collect my washing.'

'Yeh, that must be a real nuisance,' said Joe in an even voice.

Graham glanced at him. 'I need to get back.' He checked his watch. 'I want to get home before they do.'

Chapter 34

All through dinner that night Graham knew that his mum was studying him. But it wasn't until the end of the meal that she began.

'Your granda was trying to get in touch with you today. Did you know that?'

'No,' said Graham. He could imagine why though. It would be to see if he was going to come to the Walk on Saturday.

'He called me at work to say that you weren't answering your mobile.'

Graham groaned silently. 'The power's low on my mobile,' he said.

'That's not strictly true,' his mum said in a patient tone. 'I put it on the charge for you every night. Last night was no exception.'

'I think I forgot to switch it on when I left school.'

'Your granda says he called here too a few times and got no reply.'

Graham said nothing.

'Where were you after school today?'

'With friends. Nobody you know,' he added quickly to

forestall the next question.

'I know all your friends, Graham.' His mum waited, but as Graham didn't speak, she said, 'I worry if I don't know where you are. Your dad and I are concerned for you. I don't mind if you go somewhere after school but we want you to stay away from trouble.'

'Where did you go after school today, Graham?' his dad asked him in a very firm voice.

'Into the city centre,' said Graham reluctantly.

'With?'

'I met Joe.'

'Where did you go?' asked his mum.

'The music shops,' Graham lied, thinking if he told the truth and said the Gallery of Modern Art they'd never believe him.

His mum sighed. 'Why didn't you ask us first?'

''Cos you probably would've said no.'

'Well, I can't say as I like you going into the city on your own,' said his mum.

'I wasn't on my own. I was with Joe.'

'I haven't met Joe.'

'But Dad has.'

'That's not the main point,' said Graham's dad. 'You went off somewhere and we didn't know where you were. When you're young it seems a bit neurotic to always let someone know where you're going. But if something had happened to you – say a traffic accident – and you hadn't turned up for dinner tonight, we wouldn't have a clue as to your whereabouts. You're old enough to read the newspapers and see the news on TV. You know things can happen to young people when they're out on their own, just by being in the wrong place at the wrong time. I mean, there was a young man stabbed in the city centre only a few days ago.'

Graham's throat closed.

'You see where we're coming from?' said his dad.

Graham nodded. He didn't trust his voice enough to speak.

'We don't mind if you go out with your friends, even new ones like Joe that we don't know so well.'

Graham's mum frowned at this but she didn't say anything.

'We need to be told where you're going in advance.'

'And who you're with,' his mum added.

'We're not stopping you doing anything you want to do, are we?' his dad asked.

Graham didn't reply.

'Talk to me, son,' said his dad. 'We're not spoiling anything for you, are we?'

Graham shook his head.

'What is it then?'

He should tell them, Graham thought suddenly. It would be such a relief. Tears were collecting behind his eyelids. For an awful moment he thought he was going to cry. Then he remembered Leanne crying. He couldn't tell his parents. He'd promised Leanne he wouldn't.

'I – I . . .' Graham began. 'I'd like to do more things on my own.'

'Like what?' asked his mum.

'Don't know.' Graham shrugged. 'Just things. Like buy my own clothes. Maybe go with my friends to get them.

Go for a haircut myself. I mean it's nice that Dad always comes with me, but . . .'

'Fair enough,' said his dad. 'I don't mind.' He patted the top of his head where he was beginning to lose his hair. 'It lets me off the hook. I don't need to go as often as you do anyway.'

'And go out with my friends a bit more.'

'Only if you make sure you keep up with your school work,' said his mum.

'Into the city centre?' Graham knew he was pushing his luck.

'As long as it's not too late at night,' said his mum.

'I suppose we have to recognize that you're becoming an adult,' said his dad.

'Yes,' said Graham.

His mum smiled at him. 'You can plug in your own mobile phone tonight,' she said.

Graham got up from the table to leave the room.

'And with all this new-found freedom, don't be doing anything *too* daft,' his dad called after him.

Chapter 35

But he *had* done something daft.

Well, not daft exactly, more stupid. Exactly the kind of thing that his parents had warned him against. Put himself in the wrong place at the wrong time. Maybe he *wasn't* old enough to act like an adult. As Graham got ready for bed the thought was bringing him down and he tried to shake it off. Joe Flaherty was taking care of himself and his dad. He had to. If his own parents would only let the lead off then he, Graham, could be equally responsible. Part of the reason he took the dodgy short cut every Friday was to get some free time, to have some extra cash to spend, and be on his own for a little while. The way his mum flapped about doing every little thing for him annoyed him. He didn't find it helpful. It was irritating when she did things like coming into his room every night to plug in his mobile phone.

Graham sat up in bed. He'd forgotten to put his phone on the charger. He got up and rooted around in his school bag until he found it. He took it to his desk at the window and plugged it in. Looking at it made him think of Leanne. She'd have got rid of her phone by now so she didn't have to worry that it might be traced. No one knew of her connection to Kyoul. Whereas he, Graham, was probably on a CCTV camera somewhere, and despite Joe's reassurances he was uneasy. Perhaps he *should* tell his parents the whole thing and get it over with.

What would they say? What would they do? They'd call the police. Then what? He'd be grounded. For sure. Or they'd think of a suitable punishment. When he was younger they'd confiscated his computer games for a day or two; when he was older his TV or his personal stereo. Once he'd had to go straight to his room after school for a whole week. He couldn't even remember what that was for. Whatever it had been, it was nothing on this scale. For this they'd have to come up with something that really hurt. Take away something that mattered to him. The only thing that he cared about at the moment was the football.

Graham leaned forward and put his head in his hands.

They'd stop him going to the training. Even if he was picked for the team he'd be banned from playing in the tournament.

He'd just won some personal space. Won it and lost it in the same breath. He desperately wanted to play. He wanted to be chosen for the team that would represent his city. What Joe said was true. They had something. They'd won their first competitive game and beaten a team they'd expected to maul them. And it was due to him and Joe. The coach Jack Burns had noticed that they played well together. Both of them had a chance of being picked for the team. More than a slim chance. When he'd seen them playing on Sunday Joe's Uncle Desmond had pointed out that together they were strong. They might be able to do it. Represent Glasgow. Play for the city at the finals. The same turf the greats had played on – Souness, Dalglish; Pele had chosen Dalglish as one of the top one hundred football players of all time. Graham could be there, like them.

And then . . . there was Leanne and Kyoul. Graham couldn't betray them. He'd told Leanne that he'd let her know first if he decided to tell anyone, like his parents, about the situation. Giving your word was an adult responsibility. Life was full of trouble – that was what his dad had told him. It was how you handled the trouble that tested whether you were mature. He'd made the mistake of taking the short cut. Now he would have to deal with the consequences of being in the wrong place at the wrong time.

But . . . Graham raised his head and stared out of the window. The lights of the city reflected back into his room. He hadn't been in the wrong place for Kyoul.

If he hadn't been in that street, at that time, Kyoul would be dead.

In a different part of the city Joe too was being questioned.

'It's not drugs, is it?'

'Da—aad!'

Joe's dad heaved a huge sigh. 'I suppose that's a stupid thing to ask. If you were into blowing your mind there's plenty of stuff lying about this house for you to choose from without you having to buy it outside.'

'Aye,' said Joe. 'Though the street value of your sleeping tablets has fallen away, Dad. I'd get more for the anti-depressants. Nowadays folk are into uppers more than downers.'

Joe's dad put his head on one side but didn't take his eyes from his son's face.

'Mind you,' Joe went on, 'since you've been getting better and the doctor's cut your prescription, I'd not make so much. It's good that you're getting better though, Dad, isn't it?'

Joe's dad was not to be deflected. He pointed to a new CD lying on Joe's desk. 'You do seem to have more money lately.'

'I earned it, honestly.' Joe grinned at his dad. 'I earned it honestly.'

Joe's dad smiled. 'You've got the gift of the gab, I'll say that. But I'm being serious here.'

'I know fine,' said Joe. 'There's nothing to worry about.'

'My sister Kathleen and you were making with the heavy discussions on Sunday. She phoned me today and said you'll have a talk with me soon.'

Joe groaned. You couldn't trust adults, could you? 'I told her that I'd speak to you this weekend coming. I'll tell you all of it then.'

'Why not until next weekend?'

'It's when they'll pick the team and hopefully I'll be playing in the tournament. The first games are being held next Sunday. Glasgow's playing Liverpool here in Glasgow. I need to get that over before I deal with anything else.'

'Are you being bullied?'

'I'm not. Really,' Joe insisted. 'I mean, c'mon. Who would bully anybody in this family with Jammy riding shotgun?'

'Aye, right enough.' His dad continued to look at him intently. 'There's nothing I can help you with?'

Joe shook his head.

'Talk about?'

'Naw.'

'We did all thon facts of life stuff a while ago, didn't we?'

Joe nodded. 'Yeh, I think I told you everything you needed to know.'

'Ha ha.' Joe's dad leaned over and ruffled his hair. 'Too old for a hug?'

'Just a bit.'

'Well I'm not.' Joe's dad grabbed him and pulled him against his chest.

Chapter 36

For the next two days every time the classroom door opened or the phone rang at home, Graham half expected it to be the police.

He spent most of his free time in his room, using schoolwork to keep him from fretting over his planned visit to Kyoul in hospital on Thursday afternoon. His parents obviously thought he'd taken seriously their advice about adult behaviour. At one point he overheard his dad saying this to his mum, commenting on the fact that giving Graham more freedom had resulted in a more mature response to his studies.

On Tuesday night his Granda Reid came over for a visit. He had his own key for the house and was already there when Graham got in from school.

'You're later home from school tonight,' he said as Graham came into the house.

'I do supported study on a Tuesday,' Graham explained.

'Not skiving off into the town like last night?' The old man laughed. 'I'm really sorry if I got you into trouble with your mum and dad.'

'It's OK, Granda.' Graham went to the fridge to get himself a drink.

His granda's eyes followed him. 'You look a bit out of sorts,' he said. 'Are you working too hard at school?'

Graham shook his head. Here was the one person he should be able to share his worries with but he couldn't.

'I didn't come to nag you about Saturday, if that's what's bothering you.' He grinned at Graham, then added, 'Or maybe just a wee bit.'

'Oh no, Granda!' Graham exclaimed. 'It's not that.'

'So there is something?' his granda observed shrewdly.

'No, no,' said Graham. He searched for something to satisfy his granda's concern. 'The football training,' he said. 'We've got another session tomorrow. It'll be practically the last time for me to show some skills before the final selection is made.'

'Och! Is that all? Your coach would be mad not to choose you.' His granda clapped Graham on the shoulder. 'Look at you. A fine upstanding young man. When I look at you sometimes, I see myself sixty-odd year ago. You're from the best stock, Graham. Good breeding shows. And you're a thoroughbred.'

It was a speech his granda often made to Graham. The old man had been saying this to him from when he could first stand up, and in the past it'd always given Graham a warm glow to be the object of the old man's pride. But now, as he listened to his granda's familiar words, a thin thread of uncertainty entered his mind.

The next evening, Wednesday, when Graham met Joe at football training he told him of an idea he'd been turning over in his head of maybe telling his parents part of the story about Kyoul and Leanne.

'I've been thinking,' he said to Joe. 'My mum works for a firm of lawyers. Sometimes they deal with asylum cases. If I told my parents that we'd met Leanne by chance and she'd talked about Kyoul maybe they would agree to help him.'

'It's not likely though, is it?' said Joe. 'They'd want to know more.'

'I'd tell them most of it,' said Graham. 'But leave out the bit where I was in Reglan Street and went with Kyoul in the ambulance to the hospital.'

'But they'd ask where and when we met Leanne and why she spoke to us. You know what it's like when they start on at you.'

'You're right,' Graham admitted. 'And I don't think I'm very good at telling lies. My parents would see through me.'

'Me too,' said Joe. 'In fact my da had a go at me the other night. My Auntie Kathleen let him know I'd something to tell him.'

'You didn't say anything, did you?' said Graham in alarm.

'As if!'

'Please don't,' said Graham anxiously. 'If it's all going to come out I want to be the one to break the news to my parents.'

'If that happens we'll do it together, if you like.'

'Would you?' said Graham.

'Well, you got yourself into the situation. But I guess I persuaded you to go and see Kyoul in the hospital. And we're both kind of stuck with it because we gave Leanne our word that we wouldn't tell.'

'You make it seem reasonable.'

'You saved someone's life,' said Joe. 'Don't forget that. It would've been simpler to leave him.'

'I think they'll track us eventually. They'll go round the schools with the grey uniforms again.'

'I'm not so sure,' said Joe. 'Half the schools in the city have got grey uniforms. And if they had anything solid on the CCTV they would have got to you by now. Tomorrow's Thursday. We'll meet up after school and go to the hospital and give Kyoul the envelope. Then we'll see Leanne like we said, on Friday, to tell her that he got the package safely. And that'll be us definitely finished with the whole thing. Now' – Joe punched Graham on the arm – 'we've training to do with a game at the end of it, and a coach to impress so that we get chosen to play for Glasgow.'

Jack Burns was waiting for them.

'What gives with you two?' he said.

'Nothing,' said Graham and Joe together.

'Why does that worry me?' said Jack Burns. 'When boys of your age answer "nothing" to a question about what they're doing I have this deep feeling of foreboding.' He watched Joe and Graham as they ran out to warm up, glad that they seemed to be forming a friendship away from the football field. He was aware of how difficult it might be for them, given their differences in background and culture, but this vibrant mixture was the essence of Glasgow.

The training sessions had a good clutch of boys whose origins were in half a dozen or so countries of the earth, keen to play for the city. These two he'd been keeping his eye on ever since they'd turned up for training. Over the weeks some boys stopped attending as their initial enthusiasm waned, but Graham and Joe had stayed the course, if anything keener than they'd been at the start. Jack had fostered their development. Seen at once that Joe was hungry for the ball. Despite being slightly built he shrugged off tackles. Believed he could do it, always got up again, always bounced back, his determination unquenchable. And, if Joe was the fighter, then Graham was the finisher. Last Friday's goal had been an example of how exciting play could energize a game and the players. A goal scored on the run. And Graham had stamina, which was why initially he'd put him centre mid-field, but he intended to try something else tonight. Jack had restrained himself from giving too much praise after last Friday's game, even though Graham's race to the box to intercept Joe's cross and convert it to a goal had left him breathless. If he could nurture their individuality and marry it to their team play he knew that he had two stars in the making.

Graham and Joe could hardly wait the forty-five minutes for the formal part of the session to be over and it was time for the short game they usually played at the end. They weren't really surprised to find that Jack Burns had placed them on the same team again. But this time Jack moved Graham to striker position and put Joe on the left. They weren't long into the match before the combination began to show results. Joe, moving wide on the wing, cut back a cross for Graham to nod it home. The boys were ecstatic. So hyped up that they did not anticipate the counter-attack. Not surprisingly the opposition went up the park and scored almost immediately.

Afterwards Jack Burns spoke to all of them about handling success and then talked them through some set pieces. He kept his face severe but inwardly he was smiling. He would need to knock some good sense into Joe and Graham, but for the first time he was hopeful that his team would make a showing in the inter-cities tournament.

Chapter 37

On Thursday after school Graham went home to change before setting out for the hospital with Joe.

The phone was ringing as he entered the house. It was Granda Reid.

'I've had a thought about the Walk on Saturday,' he said, and continued quickly before Graham could speak. 'I'd like you to come along at the beginning and see what it's like. You don't have to actually walk if you don't want to, but I think you'd enjoy the atmosphere. And I could show you off to all my friends at the Lodge, the past Masters and the like. That's not too much to ask, is it?'

The kitchen clock was counting off the seconds. Graham needed to meet up with Joe and get to the hospital before afternoon visiting ended.

'OK, Granda,' he agreed. 'I'll come over early on Saturday morning.' Hanging up the phone, he raced upstairs. He picked out a pair of grey trousers and a jacket to wear.

Graham was now glad he'd had the upset with his parents at the beginning of the week. It meant he didn't feel he had to specifically ask them if it was OK to go into town after school today. He was sure that one of the reasons they worried about him was because he was an only child. Usually he fell in with how they organized his life. It was only recently that he'd become discontented with that. He wasn't even sure why. The way his life was he'd no big complaints. On the whole his parents were both OK. They all got on well together and went on holiday as a family every year. Graham wondered how his mum and dad had lived when they were his age. Although Granda Reid kept him well informed on the family's history, Graham had never asked about the recent past. He hadn't known that his dad used to work in the East End of Glasgow. Graham wondered what else he didn't know about his parents. He knew that they'd worked hard to buy the house. There couldn't have been much money when they were growing up. So now there came a faint inkling of what their life must have been like compared to his own. And, Graham realized, it was his meeting with Kyoul that had make him think about all this.

Before leaving his house Graham put a note on the table in the hall. He hoped to be home before his parents got in from work. If he didn't, they couldn't say he hadn't told them where he was going and who he'd be with.

Going into town with Joe for an hour or so. Will be home for dinner around six.

He added, *Don't worry*, and then scored it out. If his mum read that she would immediately wonder why he thought she might be worried.

* * *

Graham met Joe outside the City Chambers and they crossed George Square to get a bus that would take them to the City Hospital.

'We should catch the tail end of afternoon visiting,' said Joe. 'But we'll need to be quick as it's bound to be less busy on a weekday and we don't want anyone noticing us too much.'

Joe too had changed into dark casual gear and they both wore baseball caps with the skip down low. Outside the ward they stopped to discuss a plan.

Graham peered inside. 'There's one or two visitors hanging about. And the curtain's drawn round Kyoul's bed.'

Joe looked over his shoulder. 'That man I spoke to last time, Mr Sinclair, is still there in the bed next to Kyoul. So we've got a legit reason to be in the ward if anyone asks. The only thing is' – Joe grasped Graham's arm – 'he's kind of half sitting up and his eyes are open. I don't think you'll be able to slip through the curtain next his bed without him noticing.'

'I'll follow you in,' said Graham, 'but I'll go down the other side of the ward and into the toilets at the end. Then I'll walk through and slip behind the curtain there.'

'Fine,' said Joe. He handed Graham the envelope. 'I'll go straight down and sit beside Mr Sinclair. I'll keep watch for you like the last time and whistle if I see anyone approaching Kyoul's bed.'

Mr Sinclair was propped up in bed. He gave a huge smile as he saw Joe approaching him.

'I was hoping you'd come in to see me again, son,' he greeted Joe. 'Sit down. Sit down.'

Joe pulled up a chair. 'How're you doing the day?'

'No bad. No bad.'

'D'you think McMahon was worth the transfer fee?' Joe launched at once into the subject of football. 'Everybody says he reminds them of McCoist when he played for Rangers.'

Mr Sinclair shook his head. 'In my book he's more like Willie Henderson. McCoist was a goal scorer. Henderson was a winger.' He gave Joe a long look. 'Full of tricks, he was.'

'Henderson's a bit before my time,' said Joe. 'I don't know much about him.'

'That doesn't surprise me,' said Mr Sinclair. 'Did you tell your da I was asking for him?'

'Oh aye,' said Joe.

'How *is* your old man?'

'No so good,' said Joe.

Mr Sinclair nodded solemnly in sympathy. 'Probably the weather. It's that changeable the now. Does the damp get into his bones?'

Joe nodded.

'He'd need to keep himself wrapped up then,' Mr Sinclair said with a broad smile.

'Aye,' said Joe. 'He does.'

'Dinna cast a cloot till May is oot.'

'Uh. Right.' Joe looked more closely at Mr Sinclair. There was something going on here that he couldn't quite work out. Mr Sinclair seemed to have deliberately moved the conversation away from football. And he was grinning and wittering on, which made it hard for Joe to pay attention to what he was supposed to be doing, covering Graham's back. Between Mr Sinclair's questions, Joe was sure he could hear a voice behind the curtain of the next bed. Graham must have been directly behind him to get to Kyoul so fast. Joe moved his chair slightly so that he could keep a lookout all the way to the entrance door.

And saw Graham walking down the ward on the opposite side.

Joe's eyes opened wide in fright. If Graham wasn't at Kyoul's bed, who was talking behind the curtain?

He spun round in his chair. Mr Sinclair was watching him with an amused expression. Something not quite right was becoming something totally disastrous. There must be a nurse or a doctor in with Kyoul.

Joe stood up and tried to attract Graham's attention. Across the other side of the ward Graham disappeared into the toilet block.

Joe tried to whistle. His mouth was dry. He could scarcely get the sound out. Mr Sinclair stared at him.

'What're you doing, son?'

Joe realized he was whistling, '*Celtic, Celtic, that's the team for me!*'

He coughed and spluttered. 'I've got something caught in my throat,' he gasped.

'Take a wee drink of water.' Mr Sinclair indicated the water jug on his bedside cabinet.

Joe grabbed the glass. His hands were trembling. He gulped some water. Graham was heading into danger! He only had seconds to warn his friend. He tried to whistle through his teeth. Nothing but a hiss came out.

Mr Sinclair gave him a most peculiar look.

It was too late.

The doctor or nurse behind the curtain raised their voice. Not quite a yell, but enough to be heard in the main ward.

'Come back here! I want to talk to you!'

Graham must have gone behind the curtain, been seen by the person with Kyoul, and was making a run for it. He'd better do the same. Joe turned to leave.

A hand like a claw shot out and grabbed his wrist.

'Don't move!'

Chapter 38

'Sit where you are.'

Mr Sinclair's grip on Joe's wrist was surprisingly strong.

'Wha-aat?'

'No point in you both getting caught.'

'Caught?'

'Your pal might escape if he's smart off the mark. But you've no chance. If you try to run you'll not make it. Sit down quick.'

Joe eyed the ward sister walking hurriedly towards them. He sat down reluctantly. 'What am I going to say?'

'Nothing. I'll say what needs saying.'

The next moment a male nurse came out of the toilet block. 'Wee blighter got away,' he said.

'What's going on?' said the sister.

'A boy. About his age' – the male nurse pointed at Joe – 'came behind the curtain while I was dressing Kyoul's wound. He must have come through from the toilet block. I think he was trying to speak to Kyoul, but of course Kyoul claims he's never seen him before. He ran away out through the fire exit.'

The sister turned to stare at Joe. 'You were with that boy at the ward door earlier on. I saw you. Who is he?'

'Dunno,' Joe stammered. 'I met him in the lift on the way up.'

'Aw heh, don't bother the boy,' said Mr Sinclair. 'He only comes here to visit me.'

'I saw them talking together,' the sister insisted, 'as if they knew each other.'

Joe shook his head.

'Listen,' said Mr Sinclair. He beckoned to the ward sister. 'See him.' He indicated Joe. 'He's my great-nephew.' He lowered his voice. 'Nice boy an that, but no the sharpest tool in the box. The light's on upstairs but there's nobody home, if you get my drift. Knows nuthin about nuthin, ken?'

The sister nodded slowly, but continued to look at Joe. Joe tried to assume the look he frequently saw on his cousin Jammy's face.

'So you didn't know the boy who was visiting the patient in the next bed?' The sister asked Joe again.

'Naw,' said Mr Sinclair, answering her question. 'We don't. The only boy I know is this yin here.' He made a movement in the bed and gave a smothered moan. 'This pain is murder.' He let out a groan.

'Try to relax, Mr Sinclair.' The sister looked concerned. 'I'll put out a call for a doctor if you need medication.'

'You do that.' Peter Sinclair winked at Joe as the sister and the male nurse hurried away.

Joe's heart was lurching. 'How did you know . . . ?'

'That you were a fraud?'

Joe nodded.

'You mean, apart from you whistling that bampot Celtic tune a minute ago?'

'Och that,' said Joe, trying to salvage the situation. 'I heard someone humming that tune on the bus, so I did.'

'Aye, a *Septic* Celtic supporters' bus,' said Mr Sinclair, laughing. 'Anyway, I knew you weren't in here to see me.'

'What?'

'I had you sussed from the start, son.'

'You did?'

'Och aye. I was on to you the very first day.'

'How?'

'Whilst you were talking I kept thinking about you saying your dad was my pal Jimmy. The Jimmy I knew was almost thirty year older than me, so unless he was having bairns when he was seventy-two you can't be his boy.'

'His grandson?' Joe offered.

'Naw.' Mr Sinclair shook his head. 'I just minded after you left the last time. Jimmy dropped dead in the Co-op one Saturday about five year ago. Right fornenst the meat counter it was. While he was waiting to buy some mince for his dinner. Being the Co-op, it was a wee while afore anybody thought to ask why the queue wasn't moving. So you see, Jimmy's been pushing up the daisies in the Auld Aisle cemetery for the last five year. And unless he arranged to have cable piped into his coffin, he's definitely no been watching the bowls on the telly.'

'Are you going to tell anybody about me?' Joe whispered shakily.

'Who would I tell?'

'I'll no bother you any more, mister. I promise.'

'Naw naw, son. I quite like you visiting me. Your patter's great. I've no family to come and see me apart from that carnaptious sister of mine and her greetin-faced man.'

'But . . .' For once Joe was lost for words. 'But why . . . ?'

'Why did I no let on? My dad fought in the Second World War. He didn't talk about it much. But I remember him saying that after he'd seen the gas chambers, he was glad he'd fought in that war. The way I see it, it was the one war in a whole mess of wars where there was a reason to fight. And even though I was young, I understood what the fighting was for. It was so that young men like him' – Mr Sinclair jerked his thumb in the direction of Kyoul's bed – 'could grow up and live without being tortured or put in camps.'

'You know he's been tortured?'

'I've seen his scars, and I've heard how he got them.'

Joe looked away.

'Scarred outside *and* inside,' Mr Sinclair went on. 'We talk at night when there's nobody around.'

'You know by helping me it could involve you in something dodgy.' Joe cleared his throat. 'You see, Kyoul . . . He might be . . . illegal.'

'Aye. So?'

'By not telling what you know, you could get in trouble from the polis.'

'I'm that feart.' Peter Sinclair smiled at Joe. 'I'm dying of cancer, son. I've only got weeks, days maybe. What're they going to do to me? Put me in the jile?'

'Right enough,' said Joe.

'The thing is, anyway, it's kept my mind off the pain. I'm grateful, I can tell you. It's the most interesting thing that's happened since I got here.'

'What do I do now?' said Joe.

'You wait until they ring that wee bell to tell you visiting time's over,' said Peter Sinclair, 'and then you walk out of here, casual like, with all the rest.'

Graham fell into step beside Joe as he reached the bus stop.

'Never again,' he said. He handed Leanne's envelope to Joe. 'I feel bad that I didn't manage to deliver this but I am *never* going back to that hospital. If I hadn't got out through the fire door I would've been caught. And where were you when I needed you?' he demanded.

'I tried to warn you,' said Joe.

'By whistling that crap song?'

'Sorry. It was the only one I could think of.'

'I was expecting you to be right behind me. How did you get away?'

'That man,' said Joe, 'the patient I pretend to visit – Mr Sinclair – he grabbed my arm.'

'Why'd he do that?' said Graham.

'Peter Sinclair,' said Joe, 'is more all there than I gave him credit for. He told the ward sister that I was his great-nephew and then asked to see a doctor.' He paused. Should he tell Graham that Mr Sinclair had also told the ward sister that he was a bit dighted? Joe decided against it. Instead he said, 'Mr Sinclair kept them busy so you could get away.'

'Why?'

'Him and Kyoul talk during the night. He probably knows more about Kyoul than we do.'

As they got off the bus in the city centre, Joe asked Graham, 'D'you want to come for a kick-about?'

'I need to go home,' said Graham. He was still slightly frazzled. 'But my football career's over anyway. The nurses could make up an identikit photo of me. From now on I can hardly go outside.'

'Your bahoukie,' said Joe.

'Easy for you to say,' said Graham. 'The hospital will tell the police my description. I'm sure they think I'm one of the gang that did the stabbing. That male nurse got a good look at me. I'll never be able to play football in public.'

'Aye, you will,' said Joe.

Graham pointed to his face. 'I'm too well known.'

Joe put his head to one side and studied him. 'You know, there's a dead easy way to change how you look. And it only takes about an hour.'

'What?' said Graham.

'Tomorrow, when football training's over,' said Joe, 'after we meet Leanne. You've got some time to spare before you've to get home, haven't you?'

'Yes. I can't start going home earlier now. Why?'

Joe grinned at Graham.

'I have a cunning plan.'

Chapter 39

During the game on Friday evening, Graham and Joe played their hearts out.

Their team lost three–nil.

In the dressing room they stood talking.

'We played pure mince there.' Joe's voice was unsteady. 'You know Jack Burns is supposed to be making the selection tonight. We don't have a hope.'

'Keep your cool,' said Graham. 'So we didn't score. But we forced some good saves. By the end they were defending deeper and deeper.'

'Yeh' – Joe crammed his gear into his bag – 'but a game is won by goals. That's what counts in the end.'

'I think Jack Burns brought in those older boys tonight to see how we stood up under pressure. And we did well. We didn't flag or fade away. You were making chances right up to the final whistle.'

Joe felt better on hearing Graham's encouraging words. It was one of the things he liked about Graham. He was quieter than Joe, didn't act as rashly, or comment so quickly. He'd think before he gave his opinion.

Graham looked over Joe's shoulder. 'Jack Burns

is speaking to everybody individually on the way out.'

Joe's heart stuttered. 'He'll be telling them whether or not they've to turn up on Sunday.' He picked up his ruck-sack. 'I'd rather know right away. I'll wait for you outside.'

Jack Burns consulted the list he had in his hand as Joe approached him. Then he looked up and smiled. 'You're in, Joe,' he said. 'You're part of the team that's going to represent Glasgow.'

Joe said thanks and turned away after Jack told him the news. His eyes started to burn and he'd to gulp a few times before he could breathe properly. He'd wanted this so badly that he'd not allowed himself to think about it. He'd been selected! Picked for Sunday's game against Liverpool. He was playing for Glasgow! Joe leaned on the wall outside as he waited for Graham to appear. Maybe his dad would come to the game. He would ask his Auntie Kathleen and Uncle Tommy if they would take him and sit with him.

Graham came out with a jaunty look about him. He ran up to where Joe was waiting for him at the entrance to the training fields. 'I'm in! I'm in! Are you?' He gave a whoop of delight when Joe nodded. 'My mum and dad both said they'd come and watch the game on Sunday if I was selected.' Graham took Joe by the shoulder and spun him round. 'Brilliant, isn't it?'

Joe nodded again. He didn't trust himself to speak.

Graham and Joe's high spirits sagged as they went to meet Leanne in the city centre. They would have to give her back the envelope and tell her that they hadn't been able to get the information to Kyoul.

Leanne was waiting for them under the archway outside the Tron Theatre. She began to wave and smile when she saw them.

'I don't know about you,' Graham said to Joe, 'but I feel rotten. Look at her. She's dead happy because she thinks we've done it and Kyoul will be safe.'

Joe slouched his shoulders. Both boys walked a little slower.

Leanne came to meet them. 'Thank you—' she began.

'Don't,' Joe interrupted her at once. 'Don't thank us.' He handed Leanne the envelope. 'We couldn't do it,' he explained. 'It just wasn't possible . . .'

But Leanne didn't seem to have heard him. 'Thank you,' she said again. 'This is going to make such a difference. It means Kyoul has somewhere safe to stay while he makes contact with one of the asylum drop-in centres.'

'Listen,' said Graham. 'Leanne, listen to us. We didn't get the information to Kyoul. He's still trapped in the hospital.'

'But he's not.' Leanne looked at Joe. 'Your uncle gave Kyoul the keys of his flat and said he could stay there for a bit.'

'My uncle?' said Joe.

'Yes,' said Leanne. 'He is letting Kyoul stay at his house. Kyoul sneaked out of the hospital last night and was waiting for me after school. He's very weak, but much happier because he's free and able to speak to me.' She looked at Joe. 'It's really good of you to ask your uncle to let Kyoul use his house.'

'I don't know what uncle you're talking about,' said Joe.

'Mr Sinclair, in the bed next to Kyoul.' Leanne gave Joe a puzzled look. 'I thought you knew. He explained to Kyoul he was your uncle and he gave him his house keys. He told him he could stay there while he was in hospital. He said he wouldn't be using his flat for a while.'

Mr Sinclair!

The man in the bed next to Kyoul in hospital.

Mr Sinclair, who knew he was dying, had given his house keys to Kyoul. For once Joe didn't have a ready remark. He only knew that he must go back and visit Peter Sinclair again.

Chapter 40

By the time Joe got to the hairdresser's shop his Aunt Kathleen and his granny were waiting at the door.

'Where've you been, Joe?'

'Sorry,' said Joe. 'Got held up.'

'You know what time the bingo starts. And we told you it was going to be busy today. There's a mound of stuff to do.'

'It's OK,' said Joe. 'It's OK. You two go on. I'll manage. I'll phone my da and tell him I'll be later.'

'It'll take you ages,' said his granny. 'We did tell you we'd be specially busy tonight.'

'Look, son' – his Aunt Kathleen put her hand in her purse – 'take this extra money and get a taxi home.'

'Right,' said Joe. 'Just go, will you?'

'Promise me you'll take a taxi?'

'OK,' said Joe. 'OK.'

Joe waited until the two women had gone. Then he went outside and whistled – successfully this time.

Graham scuttled from a nearby close mouth into the shop.

'You're sure about this?' he asked Joe nervously.

'No bother,' said Joe, rummaging in a cupboard. He came out holding a tube of hair tint. 'I've watched my granny and Auntie Kathleen do this dozens of times.' He went behind the counter and found a bottle of peroxide. '*Sixty volume*,' he read from the label. 'That's the best stuff.'

'You're absolutely positive that you know what you're doing?' Graham asked him.

'Sure.' Joe picked up a tin marked BLEACH and emptied some of the white powder into a plastic bowl. 'By the time we're done here your own mother won't recognize you.' He sloshed in some of the contents of the bottle and mixed it up.

'Now we slop this stuff onto your head for . . . a wee while.'

'A *wee while*?' Graham queried as Joe plastered the paste onto his hair.

'Aye, aye,' Joe said reassuringly. 'No problem, no problem.'

He galloped around, sweeping and cleaning as Graham sat in the chair. 'It'll lift the dark colour of your hair a shade or two and then you'll not match the description of the boy that was with Kyoul. Dead eas—' His voice faltered. He had stopped for a moment to glance in Graham's direction. '–sy,' he finished.

'What is it?' Graham saw Joe's expression. 'What is it? What's gone wrong?'

'Em . . . nothing.' Joe's voice was a strangled yelp. 'Wait a minute!' he cried. But Graham had already twisted his chair round to face a mirror.

Both boys gazed in absolute horror at the reflection of Graham's hair.

'This is not what you said would happen!' Graham pointed to his now white-blond hair.

'It takes a while to work properly,' said Joe nervously.

'It has worked e-blinking-nuff!' yelled Graham. 'I look like, like, like—'

'It suits you,' Joe interrupted quickly.

'– a lavatory brush!' Graham finished with a shriek.

'Honest,' Joe babbled. 'Blond hair' – he tried to remember some of the things he'd heard his granny and his Auntie Kathleen come out with to their customers – 'is very attractive. It brings out the colour in your eyes. Are you going anywhere special tonight?'

'I'll kill you!' Graham shouted. 'You've bleached my whole head!'

'Naw, naw,' said Joe. 'It's called highlights. Or maybe lowlights,' he muttered under his breath. 'A few blond streaks, that's all.'

'A few blond streaks!' Graham spluttered. 'A few blond streaks, you said, and I was stupid enough to believe you!'

'It's OK,' said Joe. 'It's OK. There's another process to be applied. Toner . . . or something.' He scrabbled under the shelf behind the desk, grabbed Graham and plunged his head into a basin.

'This ought to sort it,' said Joe. 'We'll add some ash-brown tint from this tube. That'll tone it down, but you'll still be lighter . . . different.'

From the basin Graham gave a muffled croak.

Joe patted Graham's back reassuringly. 'It'll be fine,' he said. 'Trust me.'

Chapter 41

'I'll come to your match on Sunday morning,' said Joe's dad later that evening.

Joe had just told him his news about being picked for the team.

'You will?'

Joe's dad nodded. 'I'll ask your Uncle Tommy to drive up here and take me over.' He smiled at Joe. 'Tommy's a good guy. He'll keep his eye on me.'

'That's great, Dad. But if you don't feel up to it . . .'

'I'll be fine, Joe. I want to see you play. I know it's a big thing for you to be selected. You kept up the training week on week and I'm very proud of you. But it's not just that. I feel that the whole thing is so positive. The all-city football teams coming through. And you and Gregory or Graham or whatever his name becoming friends too. It's good to meet people and get to know folk from outside your immediate circle.'

'That might not be working out,' said Joe gloomily. 'He's not too chuffed with me at the moment and I'm a bit scunnered with him too.' He looked at his dad. 'You know he's not really called after a pope?'

Joe's dad raised an eyebrow. 'I had jaloused that, yes.'

'I had to make up something quick to get Jammy off his case. His real name's Graham. He supports Rangers and . . . and I happen to know he's thinking of taking part in an Orange Walk tomorrow.'

'Ah,' said Joe's dad.

'I don't think his parents want him to,' Joe went on. 'And I'm not sure he does either, but his granda's dead keen. He's been on at him for ages.'

'That's put you off him, has it?'

'I don't know,' said Joe. 'I'm a bit mixed up in my head about it. When Graham first told me he might go in the Walk I thought he was winding me up, and then we had a kind of argument. But during this week everything was OK. We both forgot about it, what with everything else that was going on. But now . . .'

'Now you think if he does take part you and him can't be friends any more?'

'Do you think we can?' Joe asked his dad.

'You have to work at friendship, Joe. Maybe you need to stand back and give your friend room.' His dad looked at Joe seriously. 'As he'll have to do the same with you.'

Joe recalled Graham's reactions when the two of them had been in the St Franciscus church last Sunday. Graham obviously thought the statues of the saints were way too much, but it hadn't changed how he'd spoken to Joe afterwards.

'But to actually march in an Orange Walk,' Joe said to his dad. 'You said that people who did that were loonies.'

'What I said appears to have drifted in translation,' said Joe's dad wryly. 'I think you'll find the word I used was "misguided". Please try not to confuse my vocabulary with that of your Uncle Desmond.'

'*Misguided* then,' said Joe.

'I personally don't like the Orange Walks,' said Joe's dad. 'They act as a magnet for the worst kind of behaviour. I've seen people wearing green and white spat upon in the city streets on the day of the main parade. But having said that, Graham seems a nice boy. So even though he's a Rangers supporter and he might take part in a Walk, it's good that you're both still trying to be friends. It gives us hope, doesn't it?'

'Did you get selected?'

Graham's mother was standing at the freezer as he came through the back door into the kitchen that night.

'Uh-huh,' said Graham.

'That's wonderful, son,' she said. 'I'm delighted for you.'

'Yeh,' said Graham briefly.

'Aren't you pleased yourself? I thought you'd be over the moon.'

'Yeh. Yeh,' said Graham, edging past her.

His mum frowned. 'You should take off those sunglasses in the house. You'll ruin your eyes if you wear them inside.'

'OK,' said Graham. He took off his sunglasses, ducking his head at the same time.

'What's up?' asked his mum.

Graham shrugged. 'Nothing.'

'Your face is all red and blotchy. It's like an allergic reaction. Let me see.' She stopped stacking the Friday groceries and came towards him.

Graham backed away.

'Will you put the hood of your jacket down?' his mum said irritably, 'so that I can have a proper look.'

At that moment Graham's dad came into the kitchen behind him. He reached over and pulled down the hood of Graham's jacket.

A shock of bright-green hair sprang up all over Graham's head.

Chapter 42

'Are you sure he'll be here?' Jammy asked Joe.

From their position beside the wall of the railway bridge under huge billboards which stood high above the street, Jammy and Joe watched the local Orange Walk drumming up in Bridgebar Park on Saturday morning.

Joe regretted telling his cousin Jammy the truth about Graham. It had happened in a moment of annoyance when Jammy had been nag-nag-nagging him. Celtic weren't playing until Sunday afternoon. So Jammy had come round to Joe's house to suggest they met up with Gregory to practise for their game on Sunday morning against the boys from the city of Liverpool. Jammy had gone on and on so much, prodding a wound that was festering inside Joe, that eventually, stupidly, Joe had blurted out the truth about Gregory/Graham and what he would be doing today.

For, despite the conversation with his dad last night, Joe was not reconciled to Graham taking part in an Orange Walk. Although, after the disaster in the hair-dresser, Joe wasn't sure if Graham would be out in public at all. Graham had gone completely spare last night. And when Joe offered to dye his hair black he wouldn't even let Joe touch it. He'd left for home not speaking to him.

Joe's feelings of guilt fuelled his anger. He realized now how much it had riled him when Graham had told him that he might take part in an Orange Walk. He thought of his dad telling him to put his football scarf away out of sight as they came through the city centre after the game last Saturday. The fact that it was unsafe to wear Celtic colours in the city when the Orangemen were allowed to strut the streets with their banners and flags was an affront to him and his people.

Joe had wanted to go and find out if Graham would actually do it. So now Joe, who wouldn't have risked venturing into Bridgebar on his own on a day like this, was stuck with Jammy, the only person daft enough to go along with him. Joe cast his eye through the ranks of the assembling marchers. He wasn't exactly sure what he was looking for. A boy with bright-green hair? A boy wearing a bowler hat? Or would Graham have managed to dye it back to his own very dark brown?

Beside Joe, Jammy gave a sudden choking intake of breath. 'I see him,' he cried. 'I see him!'

Joe followed Jammy's pointing finger and he too gasped.

'Look!' Jammy spluttered. 'Look what they've done to his head!'

Under the bright sky Graham's bald head gleamed white.

Jammy screeched with laughter. 'They've scalped him!' He made a yipping noise, cupping his hand over his mouth. 'Aieeeee! Big Chief Eat-the-Breid has taken scalp from Blue Nose! Gaun yourself! You Hun!' he shouted. 'Next time we'll paint your whole face green!'

'Shut up!' Joe banged into Jammy so hard that they both nearly toppled from the barrier. 'Shut up! I never told you about this for you to gab it to the whole world.'

'Aw but c'mon,' said Jammy. 'It's too good to let go, that one.'

Joe grabbed him by the collar. 'If you ever mention this again I'll tell everyone we know that you wet the bed.'

'I don't wet the bed.'

'So?'

'It's rubbish that. Nobody'll believe you.'

'Aye they will.'

'I'll tell them you're a liar. Everybody'll know that you're making it up.' Jammy's voice was less confident.

'An *I'll* tell them I got the story from my granny who got it from my Auntie Kathleen who does your ma's hair. I'll say your ma was having a wee greet and my Auntie Kathleen had to run and make her a cup of tea. *Boo-hoo*' – Joe put his hands to his eyes and pretended to wipe tears away; he spoke in a falsetto voice – '*boo-hoo. Kathleen I'm fair demented with our Jammy and him in the big school too. Every other night it happens. I'm changing sheets five times a week. It's nearly killing me, trying to get them washed and dried in this weather, hauling them in and out the washing machine and the dryer. And me with my varicose veins giving me jip.*'

Jammy scowled at Joe. 'Och, see you,' he said. 'You can't take a joke.'

Joe pushed his face against Jammy's. 'It's not funny.'

'OK. OK.' Jammy backed off. 'Did we come here to chuck stuff at them? Or have you changed your mind and decided to take part in this here Orange Walk yourself?'

'I'm fed up with it,' said Joe. He took the bag of water balloons Jammy had brought with him and flung it on the ground.

'Aw c'mon,' said Jammy. 'We could have a great time winding up these wombles.'

'Naw,' said Joe. 'It'd just be like the thing that I'd get lifted and then no be able to play in the match tomorrow.'

He kicked the bag viciously with his foot. 'The football's more important to me.'

Graham didn't feel too bad about his hair. Loads of people had scrubber haircuts. It would grow soon. The outside of his head wasn't important when the inside of his head was thrumming with the atmosphere surrounding him, the restlessness of the marchers, the sound of the bands tuning up.

The air sharpened with tremulous anticipation. He'd told his granda he would consider doing it this once. Just to please him. When it was over, he'd give his granda back the sash. His parents weren't too happy about the whole thing. They'd driven him over to his granda's house early this morning but hadn't changed their own Saturday outing arrangement to meet their friends. Graham had told them that if he did decide to walk with his granda it would be this one time. His father had given him an odd look when he'd said that. Then his dad had said, 'You know, Graham, you don't have to be an Orangeman to support Rangers.'

But now Graham could hear the chat all around him, the banter as friends called to each other. And he was part of it. He was making contact with their sense of purpose, absorbing that surety of identity. It didn't matter that it was to do with events that took place hundreds of years ago. People marched for all sorts of reasons. Even the word 'march' had a ring to it, an air of authority.

It was a birthright. We had a duty to do it, owed it to those who'd fought and died to protect it. It was every Briton's right. Free assembly. To walk the highway. On any road they chose. A democratic right. Won by our fathers and forefathers. The people had been walking this city since the early eighteen hundreds and they would not stop.

Granda Reid placed the sash over his head and laid it on his shoulders. The colours were glorious. That was the only way to describe them. The fringes spread thick across the new black jacket his granda had bought him. Outsiders could say that the colours were garish. They were unmistakable, that's what they were. No one who saw them would think they were anything other than what they were. And they were his. If he had been in any doubt before, he was in no doubt now. The thud of the drum matched his heartbeat.

He would march.

He would march.

Chapter 43

They sang a hymn before they moved off.

Graham didn't go in for hymn singing and he noticed a lot of the other young people were drifting about, not paying attention. The Lodge men formed a small semicircle, took off their hats and sang unaccompanied. Most of them were white-haired. Former shipyard employees, foundry men, engineering workers; veterans of the heavy industries that had made Glasgow, at one time, the second city of the Empire. Their voices lifted to the sky. In a moment of insight Graham saw this was the core of it for his granda and his friends.

Faith.

Immediately after, Granda brought his friends over to introduce them, and Graham was shaking hands with more people than he'd known in his lifetime.

'So this is him.'

'Your grandson.'

'At last.'

'Your granda talks about you all the time, son. D'you know that?'

'Dead proud of you, he is.'

'How you work so hard at school.'

'How you love the football.'

'And a great wee player too, I've heard.'

'Be playing for Scotland one day,' Granda Reid boasted.

'Sure to, if he's got your blood in his veins.'

'There's no denying his origins.'

'Looks just like you, so he does.'

At this point Graham caught sight of his granda's face. There were tears in the old man's eyes.

'Named for you, was he?'

'Naw, naw,' his granda replied. 'The other side got that. You know how it goes. First son called after the father's father. Tradition like.'

'Did you get a middle name?'

'I did that. His name's Graham John.' Granda Reid patted Graham's shoulder. 'Liz suffered her losses before she got him. Shilpit wee thing when he arrived. I remember the day he was born. I was the first to hold him, after his parents like. They were that worried about him. But I knew. I just knew he'd be fine in the end.'

'Aye, look at him, John.'

'He's your living image.'

The bands were ready. Impatient to be off.

The banners were raised high; the name of each Lodge triumphantly emblazoned.

His granda's face was flushed.

The day had been cloudy but the sun was breaking through. Silver glinted from the instruments and the medals.

'The sun shines on the righteous,' said Graham's granda. He led Graham to his place near the front of the parade. He put his hand on his shoulder.

The Orange Walk began.

His granda rhymed off the names of the streets they would walk. A roll-call of Glasgow's history: Cathedral Square, Castle Street, High Street, across the Gallowgate, Tolbooth Steeple, Glasgow Cross, London Road.

Along the side of the Cathedral.

The tramp of their feet on the cobblestones led on by the music.

Swinging into Castle Street.

The statue of King William of Orange.

'Eyes . . . LEFT!' Granda Reid's military-style command was for Graham alone. John Reid's own personal salute to King Billy.

Down the High Street. To the sound of drum and flute. Through the heart of the city.

The police had closed off one lane for them. The Walk marshals spread wide to patrol the line. They were on the main road now. Beating out their colours.

Crowds of people had come to see them. They thronged the pavements, waving, cheering, clapping them on. Some broke through the police escort. They capered alongside the marchers, brandishing flags and mini batons.

The real baton master was at the front. He led the way. Sending the long pole hurtling skywards. Twirling, spinning, bending forwards, bringing it over his back. Retrieving it with a grand flourish. The people crowding the street were delighted. They roared approval.

Round the Tolbooth Steeple. The way it stood there in the middle of the intersection meant that every lane of traffic had to stop to let them through.

The parade halted, marking time in front of the stone lion rampant on the ancient Mercat Cross.

They wheeled round, slow marching on the inside, to make the turn into London Road.

On the corner of the Gallowgate, Joe's granny's shop.

The window shutter was pulled down. Graham remembered that Joe's family said they closed up when the Orange Walks went past. With a name like Flaherty above the shop door it was probably wise.

Joe's Aunt Kathleen was standing at the door. Kathleen with the open laughing smile who'd welcomed him into her home, asked no questions, made dinner for him.

Graham couldn't read the expression on her face.

He looked at his granda. His granda, so tall that, despite being a good height for his age, Graham had to look up at him.

Granda Reid's eyes were shining. He was staring straight ahead.

He didn't see what Graham saw.

The look on Kathleen's face.

Her turning away, going inside the shop.

The door closing.

Chapter 44

Jammy was in a bad mood.

He scuffed his feet and kept his head down, muttering to himself as he followed Joe away from the streets of Bridgebar and into the city centre.

'I'm going to Auntie Kathleen's house,' he announced as the boys neared Glasgow Green.

'Good idea,' said Joe. He knew his Aunt Kathleen would be at the shop. But maybe his Uncle Tommy would be in and he could unload Jammy on him.

His Uncle Tommy opened the door. 'Going to see the Jags today?' Joe asked him. His uncle was wearing his Partick Thistle scarf.

'I am that.'

Tommy looked at the boys. 'Why don't you both come with me?' he asked them. 'My treat.'

'Great,' said Jammy at once.

'I'm taking the car,' said Tommy. 'But I'll have to do a big detour round the city to get there. There's a Walk on, so the traffic will be held up.'

'We know,' said Joe quickly before Jammy could say anything. He gave Jammy a warning glare. He knew that Jammy would not be able to keep his mouth shut for long about Gregory really being Graham and taking part in today's Orange Walk. But hopefully it would be a few days before Jammy told anyone.

'You coming, Joe?' His Uncle Tommy was looking at him.

Joe shook his head. 'I think I'll just go home,' he said.

'Go up through the Calton then.' Tommy glanced at his watch. 'The Walk will be at the Cathedral by now. You can cut across behind them. Best to avoid that whole area around Glasgow Cross today.'

'OK,' said Joe.

His uncle opened his car door. 'Straight home now,' he said.

'Right.' Joe waved as Tommy drove off with Jammy sitting beside him in the front.

He began to walk towards the Calton to take the long way home. Then he stopped.

Why should he?

It was his city.

Why should it be that on certain days he was made to feel unwelcome? That he'd no right to be here? As if, on all the other days, he was only being tolerated. As if he didn't truly belong?

Joe turned towards the city centre.

He heard them first. You always did.

The crashing noise of the drums, the mingled yells of the onlookers.

They were marching in a loop. Coming from the

streets near Bridgebar, up to the Cathedral, down the High Street, back along London Road.

Ahead of him in the Gallowgate Joe saw his granny pulling down the steel shutter of the shop. He dived across the road to the other side. If she spotted him she'd call him inside. And she'd tell his dad later that she'd caught him on the streets near the Orange Walk. Something he'd been warned against.

Joe went towards Glasgow Cross. He *would* walk up the High Street. As he was entitled to do.

Round the Tolbooth the crowd was denser. Packing the streets. Joe scowled and determinedly elbowed his way through.

At the kerbside a big policeman viewed Joe with a shrewd gaze.

'Where are you going?'

'Nowhere,' said Joe.

'Ask a stupid question,' said the policeman, under his breath. 'You'd be better off out of here for the next hour or so.'

'Why?' said Joe.

The sound of the music was getting louder. The piercing cry of the flute, the aggressive banging of the drums.

'What makes you think I don't want to cheer them on?' Joe waved his arms about. 'Like everybody else here?'

The policeman shook his head. 'Son, don't go there. Away home now. It'll be over soon and then we can all get on with our lives.'

Joe backed off. He slipped behind the people lining

the road and began to make his way up the High Street.

Little children stood with their parents and grand-parents. Many held mini batons or flaunted the flag with the Red Hand of Ulster. Along the way youths grouped together; some drank from concealed bottles and cans.

Despite the smiles, for Joe the atmosphere was raw with unsettled tension. From a window a homemade banner proclaimed loyalty to the Protestant Boys.

The Celtic shop had its shutters down. Gobbets of spit clung to the steel surface.

As Joe reached the intersection with Duke Street the traffic had come to a complete standstill. He noticed a group of brightly dressed African women waiting to cross. Tourists? Asylum seekers? What did *they* make of it? he wondered.

The marchers were drawing close. Sections of the crowd got wilder. Singing. Chanting. Coarse words battered the air.

It stirred Joe.

Awaking a response centuries old.

He stopped walking. He bunched his fists deep in his pockets.

Moved to the edge of the pavement.

There was a hand on his shoulder. Joe glanced up, half expecting to see the big policeman. But it was his father.

'I was looking for you, Joe,' his dad said.

'Who grassed on me?'

Joe sat opposite his dad at their kitchen table.

Joe's dad laughed at his question. 'If you mean who was the concerned relative who was watching out for your welfare, then I guess you could blame your Uncle Tommy. He called me on his mobile.' He gave Joe an amused look. 'It seems Jammy told him all about your exploits this morning. Tommy was a bit anxious that perhaps you were going home by the shorter route.'

'And you came out of the house on your own and all the way down to get me?' said Joe.

'I surprised myself,' Joe's dad said. 'But then if I let anything happen to you, your mother would haunt me for the rest of my life.'

'I thought she was doing that already,' said Joe before he could stop himself.

His dad's hand paused in mid air, his coffee cup on its way to his mouth.

'Sorry,' Joe said at once. 'Sorry, Dad. I didn't mean—'

'No. No. Don't worry. You're right. You're right.' Joe's dad swallowed some coffee and smiled at him. 'It'll take a while. But I'm getting there. Like our city. Some things have got to be done bit by bit.'

Chapter 45

'It was an accident. I swear it,' said Joe. 'I didn't know what I was doing.'

Joe had been shadowing Graham in the dressing room since he'd arrived at the football fields on Sunday, apologizing every two minutes.

Graham put on his football boots and continued to ignore him.

'It was nothing to do with you being in the Orange Walk. Honest. I thought the colour would come out as blond streaks. It was to help you change your appearance so you could play football in public. I'm *really* sorry about your hair.'

Joe had said it over a dozen times but Graham still wouldn't answer him.

'Really, really sorry,' he said again. And then, with the beginning of irritation in his voice, he went on, 'I'm making a big gesture here, you know. I saw you in that Orange Walk yesterday, and you might not realize it, but it hacked me off. Like, seriously hacked me off. So the least you could do is speak to me.'

Graham glanced at Joe, but then looked away again quickly.

Joe slumped down on the bench.

Graham began to lace up his boots. He'd told Joe last week that he'd been thinking of taking part in yesterday's Orange Walk. How could he be sure that Joe hadn't meant to turn his hair green?

Joe, watching Graham, saw the doubt on his face. He recalled his dad talking about the nature of friendship.

'I'll make you an offer,' he said. 'If it would help you feel better I'll dye my hair orange.'

Graham's eyes flickered.

'I will,' Joe said seriously. 'I'd get my Auntie Kathleen to do it. I'd tell her it was for a fancy dress at the school, like Hallowe'en or something. I'd really do it. I would.'

Graham swivelled to face him. 'Why?' he demanded. 'Why would you? It's not as though we're best pals or anything. It's not as though we go about together.'

'I still would do it.'

'Why?' Graham repeated the question. 'We only ever meet up here on the football team.'

'That's why,' said Joe.

Graham raised his eyebrows.

'Because of the team,' said Joe. 'Because of the football. When we play on the same side we're two good players. That's not boasting. You know it and I know it. For me, nothing else matters. We work together like magic. On the field, I know what you're thinking, and you seem to sense what I intend to do. Don't you?'

Graham didn't answer.

'When we play on the same team it's special, isn't it?' Joe insisted.

Graham nodded. 'I guess,' he said.

'We're playing for Glasgow,' said Joe. 'That's what's important.'

'Yes,' said Graham.

'And that's the reason I tried to change your hair,' said Joe. 'Because you were so scared at being recognized in public I thought you might not play for the city.' He looked into Graham's face. 'You've got to believe that. After all we've been through together, you've got to believe that.'

'OK,' said Graham.

Joe sat back in relief.

'But I've been thinking about that whole situation,' said Graham. 'If it turns out that Kyoul is no longer in danger of being arrested and deported then I might tell someone what happened in Reglan Street. I want to do it,' he went on, 'because, when it was reported in the newspapers that an asylum seeker got stabbed, the police asked for the witness. If no one comes forward, then it looks like Glasgow doesn't care. And that's not true. So you see the reason I must speak up.'

Joe waited until they were kitted up to go out, then he said, 'Did your parents go mad?'

'Actually no,' said Graham. 'My dad thought it was hysterically funny and eventually my mum had to laugh as well.'

'Who shaved your head?'

'My mum got someone she knew to come to the house

and do it. She said that she thought Granda Reid would have a stroke if he saw me. And even though neither her nor Dad approve of his Orange sympathies, she said she wasn't going to be responsible for him ending up in coronary care.'

'You know . . . it kinda suits you,' said Joe.

Graham punched Joe's shoulder, possibly a bit harder than was necessary. 'Aye, right.'

Jack Burns lined up his team to give them his pre-match talk.

'This is it, boys. I've talked the training. You've done the training. Now it's time to do the business. Play fair. Play fine.' He paused. 'But give no quarter.' He laughed. 'Seriously, this is the beginning of the Inter-Cities Gold Cup tournament. Today, all over the United Kingdom, boys are playing for their city. And it's a beginning for us. Your big day.

'It's also another day,' he went on. 'It's the day after an Orange Walk and a week after an Old Firm game. More games, more Walks coming up. Tension building in the city. The League Championship still to be settled this afternoon, and the Cup Final at the end of the month is between Rangers and Celtic. By which time the Walk season is in full swing. I know there are strong feelings here.'

Joe stared off into space. Graham risked a quick glance at their coach. Jack Burns didn't seem to be looking at them in particular.

'So I want you to shake one another by the hand because you are a team. Put all personal differences aside. You are a city team. From all parts of the city.'

Graham and Joe looked at each other.

'I'm asking you,' said Jack Burns. 'I'm not begging you. I'm asking you as young men to behave like grown men . . . in some cases better than grown men.'

Jack went down the line and shook each player by the hand. The team shuffled around and shook each other's hands. Graham shoved his hand at Joe, and Joe shook it quickly.

Jack Burns stood looking at them. 'We know what this city is, and what it does. And sometimes we pretend it's not happening. Who's to say that's not the way to deal with it? Maybe we should ignore all the conflict and hope it goes away. If people don't hear about certain things they won't go seeking revenge and make matters worse. Or maybe we should all talk more openly. I don't know. I'm a simple man. All I know is football. I'm here because I love football. You're here because you love football. And I'm proud of *our* city. It is our city. Because *we* are the city. So let's hear it for Glasgow City.

'*Glasgow City!*' he shouted at the top of his voice.

'*Glasgow City!*' his team shouted back.

'Right, off you go. Play the game of your lives.'

From the dugout Jack Burns watched as the boys ran out onto the park.

'You are Glasgow.' He spoke under his breath. 'You are Glasgow City.'

ACKNOWLEDGEMENTS

The author would like to thank the very many people – with their very many opinions – who have helped her with this book.